RADICAL ADVICE FROM THE ULTIMATE WISEGUY

RADICAL ADVICE FROM THE ULTIMATE WISEGUY

Solomon's Up-to-Date Insights
for Young People

LORRAINE PETERSON

BETHANY HOUSE PUBLISHERS
Minneapolis, Minnesota 55438

Illustrations by Hugo Rangel and José Martinéz

Published by Bethany House Publishers
A Division of Bethany Fellowship, Inc.
6820 Auto Club Road, Minneapolis, Minnesota 55438

Printed in the United States of America

Library of Congress Cataloging-in-Publication Data

Peterson, Lorraine.
    Radical advice from the ultimate wiseguy / Lorraine Peterson.
        p.   cm.
    Includes bibliographical references.
    Summary: Presents devotional readings for teenagers, based on the wisdom of King Solomon as expressed in the Book Proverbs.

    1. Bible. O.T. Proverbs—Meditations.
2. Teenagers—Prayer-books and devotions—English.
3. Teenagers—Religious life.
[1. Bible. O.T. Proverbs—Meditations.   2. Prayer books and devotions.
3. Christian life.]
I. Title.
BS1465.4.P47   1990
248.8'3—dc20   90-41692
ISBN 1-55661-141-2   CIP
                                                            AC

Acknowledgments

In shaping this book, I'd like to acknowledge my debt to the following reference volumes: *The New Age Cult; Proverbs: Practical Directions for Living; Proverbs: A Self-Study Guide; Proverbs: A Commentary on an Ancient Book of Timeless Advice; The Bethany Parallel Commentary on the Old Testament.*

The person who works behind the scenes on my books to smooth out the awkward sentences, to catch inconsistencies in logic, and to offer many usable suggestions is my editor—David Hazard. He is a man of unusual talent and insight who really deserves to have his name in bold-face print. As I write, I also appreciate the constant support and affirmation of my family: my father, my stepmother, my sister, Lynn, my brother-in-law Earl, and my nieces and nephews, Beth, Brett, Kaari, and Kirk. I'd also like to thank the Perez family, Juanita, Sergio, and Magdalena, whose help in getting me settled in a new city literally made it possible for me to complete this manuscript on time. Above all, I sense the love and the faithfulness of the God whose "compassions never fail" because "they are new every morning."

I realize that my hearing just the right sermon, reading the appropriate book, or experiencing story material just at the time I need it for my writing is His special miracle.

> Give thanks to the Lord, call on his name; make known among the nations what he has done. Sing to him, sing praise to him; tell of all his wonderful acts. Glory in his holy name; let the hearts of those who seek the Lord rejoice. Look to the Lord and his strength; seek his face always. Remember the wonders he has done. (Psalm 105:1–5)

About the Author

LORRAINE PETERSON was born in Red Wing, Minnesota, grew up on a farm near Ellsworth, Wisconsin, and now resides in Ciudad Juarez. She received her B.A. (in history) from North Park College in Chicago, and has taken summer courses from the University of Minnesota and the University of Mexico in Mexico City.

Lorraine has taught high school and junior high. She has been an advisor to nondenominational Christian clubs in Minneapolis public schools and has taught teenage Bible studies. She has written several bestselling devotional books for teens:

If God Loves Me, Why Can't I Get My Locker Open?
Falling Off Cloud Nine and Other High Places
Why Isn't God Giving Cash Prizes?
Real Characters in the Making
Dying of Embarrassment & Living to Tell About It
Anybody Can Be Cool, But Awesome Takes Practice
If the Devil Made You Do It, You Blew It!
Radical Advice From the Ultimate Wise Guy

Contents

Were Do We Begin?

A Christian youth worker can tell you that too many of today's teenagers lack a knowledge of basic biblical values. Few know enough of God's Word to discern that situational ethics, reincarnation, Eastern meditation, or man's evolution from energy into a little god is inconsistent with divinely revealed truth. Things like transparent honesty, sexual purity until marriage, responsibility, glorifying God by being a good worker, and submission to authority are seen as outmoded standards from another generation. When young people accept Christ, it is not safe to assume that they know the difference between right and wrong.

Not long ago I counseled with a tearful teenaged girl who professed to be a Christian but whose life was totally messed up. She was not hard and rebellious, but because of weak role models, poor examples set by Christians, and a lack of biblical foundation, she lived with a foggy confusion about right and wrong. No one had ever taken the time to methodically teach her what Scripture has to say about morals and daily conduct.

But clear standards for deciding right and wrong do exist in the Bible. I'm not talking about lists of do's and don'ts. I mean biblical *principles* that a maturing young person can take in hand and begin to apply to life's real and difficult situations—principles that activate the work of God's Holy Spirit in everyday life. And once my young friend got ahold of some of these principles, her life began to change radically for the better.

There is one book of the Bible that contains *the* most practical guidelines for putting your faith to work in everyday life, a book that is specifically directed to young people: that, of course, is Proverbs. To me, it's an easy-access mine, supplying a treasure of wisdom about

11

life, relationships, work, worshiping God, and how to gain self-control in a world where there are almost no controls and so many personal heartaches. Learning to be wise in a foolishly permissive society is a top priority, especially for the young man or woman who has so many future-forming decisions at hand.

If you, as a young person, want to avoid worldly philosophies that lead to hurt and frustration, if you want to get the most out of each day, and if you are to enter the kingdom of heaven, you can find your way by starting with this solid truth: "The fear of the Lord is the beginning of wisdom."

Have You Opened the Right Door?

Real biblical Christianity differs from every other religion on earth in that it is a relationship with the Savior of the world—not a system of good works, meditation, or ritual to attain a certain spiritual goal. The idea that we can earn our way to Heaven, or Paradise, or Nirvana appeals to our pride—it makes us feel as if we're better than those who don't try and that we're in control of our destiny. However, it also brings stress and slavery: When are you sure you've done enough? What if others are doing more than you are?

There is one sure door to friendship with God the Father, and that is in opening up your heart to Jesus Christ, God's Son, who said: "I *am* the gate; whoever enters [God's presence] through me will be saved" (John 10:9). The Bible clearly states that all our attempts to come before God and insist on our own goodness apart from Christ are futile (see Isaiah 64:6). "All have sinned and fall short of the glory of God" (Romans 3:23). We're all sinners and we cannot save ourselves. Sin isn't just murder, rape, and robbing banks—it's the attitude of self-sufficiency that says, "I don't need God" or sometimes, "I'll be my own god, thank you."

Scripture further explains that no person can live up to God's standards, so He sent Jesus, who had no sin, to suffer the penalty of separation from God that you and I deserve. Jesus experienced death and hell for us—but He arose from the grave and today He sits at the right hand of God the Father and prays for us! He *wants* to see us win the fight of faith!

Your part is to "believe in the Lord Jesus, and you will be saved" (Acts 16:31). Eternal life is a gift that you receive by faith. The Bible emphasizes: "For it is by grace you have been saved, through faith—and this not from yourselves, it is the gift of God—not by works, so

13

that no one can boast" (Ephesians 2:8, 9).

Maybe you're saying, "Just believe? That's too simple." Although it's true that "the blood of Jesus . . . purifies us from every sin" (1 John 1:7), and there is nothing you can do to cover your sin, truly believing in Jesus means surrendering your whole life to Him.

Trusting Jesus means that you stop trusting in yourself and you begin letting Him help to determine your decisions and your actions. Our Lord lays down the conditions: "If anyone would come after me, he must deny himself and take up his cross daily and follow me" (Luke 9:23). That includes standing up for Jesus in the face of ridicule and opposition: "If you confess with your mouth, 'Jesus is Lord,' and believe in your heart that God raised him from the dead, you will be saved. For it is with your heart that you believe and are justified, and it is with your mouth that you confess and are saved" (Romans 10:9, 10).

Believing that Jesus is the Son of God means accepting *His* definition of sin. It means saying, "You're right, Lord, and I'm wrong." It means repenting of everything He disapproves of and changing the way you live. Repenting is turning around and going in the other direction. Jesus' word to a person who wanted a new life was, "Go now and leave your life of sin" (John 8:11). It implies that from now on Jesus is number one in your life—the only Person whom you'll ultimately obey. And you'll find His commands in the Bible.

Now you're probably worrying, "But, I don't have the power to live that way." And that's the point exactly. The Bible declares, "The righteous will live by faith" (Romans 1:17).

If you believe in and totally follow Jesus, if you ask Him to forgive your sin and come into your life, a miracle occurs. The Spirit of Jesus enters your heart and Jesus lives the Christian life through you.

If the desire of your heart is to truly believe in Jesus so that you can have a relationship with Him, pray a prayer like the following to invite Christ to be your Savior. (The words aren't magic; it's your heart attitude that God sees and honors.)

> Dear Jesus, I agree with you that I have sinned. Right now I stop confiding in my own efforts to save myself. I believe that you died on the cross for me and that only your blood can take away my sins. I repent of my sins and ask you to forgive me. I invite you to come into my heart and live your life through me. I want you to be my Savior and my Lord—the Person who is always first in my life. I promise to give up the things that you and your Word call sin and to

love and obey you all of my life. Thank you for coming into my life like you promised.

If you prayed this and meant it, Jesus is living inside you right now. He promised: "Here I am! I stand at the door and knock. If anyone hears my voice and opens the door, I will go in" (Revelation 3:20). And He would never lie.

And that is not the end of it. Jesus will begin to help you sort out right from wrong in every situation. He'll stay at your side when things get confusing. If you have faith that God can cure your loneliness and fill your longing for love, you won't "need" to have sex with your boyfriend or girlfriend. If you trust God for your sense of significance, you won't be Larry-Loud-Mouth or Know-It-All-Nora. God can also give you the power to swim against the current when someone teaches you that the Bible is full of myths.

How can you be sure you're hearing God's voice? By turning to the Bible daily. "The Bible was . . . written to show the transformed sinner how to live a life pleasing to God, now that he is saved. This instruction is . . . found throughout Scripture, but it is the *main* theme of particular Bible books. Proverbs is one of them."[1]

Proverbs without Jesus' power is a bummer. But relying on His strength within you to put His teaching into practice—it's awesome! I pray that the down-to-earth insights for living the Christian life given in this book will be the radical advice you need.

---

[1]Irving L. Jensen, *Proverbs: A Self-Study Guide* (Chicago: The Moody Bible Institute, 1988), 1.

Part One

The Wise Man and the Foolish Man

CHAPTER 1

The Secret

When Lisa studied the geography of Asia in seventh grade it was pretty boring. The name Nepal stuck in her mind only because it was the answer to a question she missed on the first-semester final.

Now, years later, Lisa couldn't believe it: She was falling in love with a handsome medical student from Nepal. Prem Shrestha was the finest Christian young man she'd ever met.

His father had been the first Christian in their province. He'd served time in prison for leaving the Hindu religion. As a child, Prem and his brothers and sisters had been cruelly persecuted. They were treated as social outcasts and were not permitted to use the village well.

Eventually, the people in Prem's town accepted the fact that he and his family were Christians and there was no more trouble—until a neighbor came to his father and wanted to accept Christ. Prem's father led the man to Jesus, and both of them landed in jail. Standing against such odds had formed in Prem the character of Christ. He was willing to live completely for Jesus—or to die for Him. Nothing else really mattered. Miraculously, God had supplied the means for him to study in India and now in the U.S. As a doctor he'd have the best possible chance to witness for Christ in Nepal.

After they had dated for six months, Prem said to Lisa, "I've been praying for the wife God has for me, and I believe you're the one. I've consulted with my parents and they're in agreement. If your father and mother give their permission, I'm willing to wait as long as I need to, because I know you'd like to go to college. I'm asking you to share a very dangerous and difficult life, and adjusting to a different culture won't be easy. Unless you're certain that God has called you, life in Nepal will be more than you can handle."

19

Lisa was awed—and troubled—by the enormity of what he was asking. But Prem's unselfishness, his sense of purpose, and the willingness to let her make her own decision made her love him more than ever. She wanted to learn everything about his country.

She found Nepal on every map. She learned to say *namaste* (hello), and *kasto cha* (How are you?). She read everything about Nepal she could get her hands on. But her best source of information was Prem. She watched him eat and noticed that he never used his left hand for anything, so she started practicing. She decided to dress more conservatively, since in Nepal everything has to reach the ankles. She just couldn't learn enough! She wanted to be the best ambassador for Christ in Nepal and the kind of wife Prem could be proud of.

Nepal was no longer a boring subject in a textbook—it became the new home that Lisa longed for.

Asking God to Meet Legitimate Needs

Lisa's attitude toward learning about Nepal changed after her heart was captured by a fine young Nepalese.

Do you find the Bible boring? Your attitude about searching the Bible for wisdom will change when you fall in love with Jesus. Your greatest need is to get to know Jesus better. Maybe your prayers are so filled with "bless me and my family," "help me on the algebra test," and "please make Matt (or Mattie) like me" that you never ask for a closer relationship with Jesus and you never spend extra time with Him.

Dear God, I want to get to know you better. I want to delight in your every word. Show me yourself.

☑ Getting the Facts Straight

Proverbs begins with the promise that all who seek God's wisdom will find *insight, discipline, knowledge,* and *understanding,* even in life's most difficult situations (see Proverbs 1:1–6). But "wisdom" is not a faceless substance—it actually has a personality and a name!

In the New Testament, Paul tells us: "My purpose is that . . . they may know the mystery of God, namely Christ, in whom are hidden all the treasures of wisdom and knowledge" (Colossians 2:2, 3). Knowing Jesus in a real and intimate way is the key to *absorbing* His wisdom. As Jesus becomes more and more real, as you search out His advice and take to heart all He says, you'll start to enjoy the *benefits* of His wisdom.

☑ Rethinking the Situation

Lisa had just returned from seeing the beautiful home her new-lywed friends Keri and Tom were building. Mentally, she contrasted the lush green carpet, the European kitchen cupboards, and the huge Jacuzzi in the master bath against the small, meager house she and Prem would have in Nepal. Doubts started to plague her. Sure she loved Jesus. Sure she wanted to be a missionary. Plus she didn't think she could exist without Prem. But living over a hundred miles from the nearest hamburger joint, never being able to watch an American TV program, and having to say goodbye to her family seemed too big a price to pay. Why couldn't they just settle down in Texas?

Later that day the doorbell rang. It was Prem, smiling as always. When he asked her what was troubling her, she told him everything. "Your happiness is more important to me than mine," he said quietly. "I'll never try to persuade you to marry me. I know that God's will for me is to return to Nepal, and I have to put God first—no matter what it costs."

As she looked into his eyes, Lisa realized that doing God's will and marrying a Christian of Prem's caliber was much more important than a living room rug, hamburgers, and TV programs.

▶ Putting the Truth Into Practice

It's so easy to lose sight of your goal, which is getting to know Jesus better and absorbing more of God's wisdom. Busyness, laziness, addiction to creature comforts—any number of things can push Jesus out of the center of your life.

Knowing Him takes effort. In addition to your regular devotional times, schedule specific dates to be with Jesus. Take a whole afternoon or evening at least once a month, and find a quiet place where you can open your Bible and let Jesus speak to you. Tell Him your secrets and ask His advice. Confess your sin and sit quietly in His presence, receiving His love.

As you cultivate a deep, intimate relationship, His words will come alive; you'll be willing to pay the price to follow Him.

His wisdom will unlock more and more of life's challenges and secrets for you.

CHAPTER 2

Observing the "No Fishing" Sign

Dave's family was new in Colorado, and he had always wanted to go trout fishing in the mountains. Because his parents were committed Christians, they didn't want him hanging around with guys who drank—which included three of the fellows who invited him to go on a weekend fishing trip. When he asked if he could go along, the answer was a resounding no.

Dave had practically grown up in the church, and he'd heard a hundred Sunday school lessons entitled "Children, obey your parents." Only six months before, a youth retreat speaker had concentrated on the problems you bring into your life by doing end-runs around parental authority. He even had to admit that his parents were godly, caring and reasonable. More than once friends of his had commented, "I wish my folks were like yours."

But this time Dave wanted his own way. After all, wasn't God a pretty easy-going guy who would overlook his breaking a few commandments? Weren't his parents too strict, and the people at church too concerned about *always* obeying God? He wanted to live a little. Besides, he wasn't joining a motorcycle gang—he just wanted to go fishing!

So Dave concocted his scheme. With his parents' permission he arranged to spend the weekend with Blake, a Christian from a different church. At school on Friday, Dave told Blake he couldn't come after all, and sneaked off to go fishing. Not wanting to appear weird, he even brought along a few cans of beer.

How do you think the story ends?

1. They get into a car accident and Dave tells his parents the truth from a hospital bed.

2. Dave's best friend from Nevada comes for a visit, so Dave's parents call Blake's house.

3. Dave gets by with lying and becomes a first-class hypocrite.

4. Dave's parents are suspicious when he returns and aren't totally satisfied with his answers to their questions. They no longer assume that their son tells the truth, and that puts a lot of strain on their relationship.

When you face a similar temptation, remember that no lie has a good ending.

THIS WAY OUT

✔ Asking God to Meet Legitimate Needs

You can grow up in the church and know all the right behavior. But unless you have that deep respect and holy sense of awe for each command of God, you'll rationalize your way into sin. Today, real respect is almost unknown: People poke fun at the President, criticize the pastor, mock their parents and ignore their teachers. A basic need of your spiritual life is true respect and reverence for God and every word He has spoken.

Dear God, teach me the true meaning of Proverbs 1:7: "The fear of the Lord is the beginning of knowledge." Show me how to worship you and stand in wonder at your holiness. Help me realize how important it is for me to obey every word you caused to be recorded in your Bible.

☞ Getting the Facts Straight

The book of Proverbs takes nine chapters to tell you how to hear and heed the instruction of wisdom. Why does Solomon spend nearly one-third of his time on one topic? It's because "commands and exhortations about daily conduct are meaningless to one whose heart attitude is not right before God."[1]

People with stubborn pride in their hearts cite biblical references to "prove" New Age doctrine, to condone immorality, to consider their race superior—but mostly to justify the sin they wish to commit at the moment. If you're not *willing* to do God's will no matter what, then you will also rationalize Scripture and imagine a God who doesn't mind if you break a few of His commandments. But, if you submit to God's laws instead of using His words to justify what you want to do and what you wish to believe, you'll be able to say with the Psalmist: "I run in the path of your commands, for you have set my heart free" (Psalm 119:32).

☞ Rethinking the Situation

Dave didn't enjoy the fishing trip as much as he thought he would. He only drank a couple cans of beer on Friday night, but it was enough to give him a headache Saturday morning. It rained all weekend and he came down with a bad cold. Of course, he had to give away the three fish he caught. He didn't get home until 10:00 P.M. on Sunday, and it was pretty obvious that he hadn't gone to the evening service with Blake.

His parents didn't say anything, but Dave felt guilty and uneasy. He had a hard time going to sleep that night. Somehow he felt more lonely than ever before. God seemed a million miles away, and Dave knew that was the result of breaking God's commandments.

For weeks Dave was depressed. He noticed his parents' distrust. They asked more questions and were less quick to give him their permission. Finally, he became so miserable he decided to confess. At the supper table one night, he cleared his throat before blurting out, "I went on that fishing trip. I'm sorry. Please forgive me."

"We know," his parents answered in unison. "But," his mother continued, "we just prayed that God would make you miserable until you confessed."

They talked for a while, and Dave said, "I sure feel a lot better

---

[1]Irving L. Jensen, *Proverbs* (Chicago: The Moody Bible Institute, 1976), 27.

now that I'm not trying to cover up a sin."

"But more than that," his dad added, "we want you to realize that you can never break one of God's commandments without suffering terrible consequences in your spirit."

☑ Putting the Truth Into Practice

Always keep your heart open to God's inspection and repent of every bad attitude He shows you. "Above all else guard your heart, for it is the wellspring of life" (Proverbs 4:23).

There are girls who sleep with their boyfriends, and give glowing testimonies in church. There are guys who do dope on Saturday, and pass the collection plate on Sunday. Some kids memorize Scripture by the yard, and cheat in school. Don't join their ranks!

Conform *your* life to what God says. After all, He knows what He's talking about.

CHAPTER 3

The Neglected Treasure

Trudy's English assignment was to write a story with an O. Henry kind of surprise ending. She thought that writing about a foolish decision and its consequences might make a good plot. So she began:

Mark's grandfather was seriously ill. The doctor gave him only a month to live. Although Mark was only twenty, he'd lost both his parents, and was his grandfather's only heir. He loved his grandfather, a man of intelligence, integrity and generosity, who was respected—even if he was considered a little odd because of his unconventional ideas.

Mark was called to his grandfather's bedside. "This piece of paper," he told Mark, "is worth at least three million dollars. It was given to me by my grandfather. It's a map of the farm he homesteaded in South Dakota before moving the family to Virginia. Remember when we drove there two years ago and I pointed out a certain spot to you? Well, this X marks that location. It's the place where he hid the gold that *his* grandfather brought back from the gold rush of 1849. Each father has insisted that his children take only part of it so some could be saved for the next generation. But the way the world is going, there may be no next generation. So I want you to take it all and invest it wisely."

Mark thanked his grandfather, even though his story sounded farfetched and he feared that his mind was going. He put the map in his top desk drawer as he rushed off to keep his date with Jacqueline. He was madly in love with her and getting her to marry him was all he could think about.

When his grandfather died a few days later, Jacqueline stayed by Mark's side. She was his only source of love and comfort and help now. Mark wanted to get married right away but Jacqueline's

27

parents said she was too young to marry and that she needed to wait a couple more years.

Two things began to torment Mark. First, he became obsessed with the fear of losing Jacqueline. He called her every day before he went to work, and drove her to her house every night. His jealousy grew. If Jacqueline talked to another fellow, Mark became upset. If she went out with her girlfriends, he worried.

Second, Mark began to fret about that treasure. What if his grandfather wasn't senile after all? The problem was, he was afraid to leave Jacqueline to go and check it out.

Because keeping up his grandfather's house took time away from Jacqueline, he hired a cleaning lady, Mrs. Smith. She came twice a week to put things in order and prepare some food he could heat up in the microwave.

One evening it took Jacqueline a long time to answer his knock. When she finally appeared and Mark suggested they go into the backyard to play badminton, Jacqueline came up with fifteen objections.

"It's just because I always beat you," Mark teased. "I'll go out and set it up and by that time you'll change your mind."

Before she could stop him, Mark ran out onto the patio, where he saw three dozen long-stemmed roses. The card said, "To Jacqueline, from Kyle Smith." He was too stunned to react.

But the coming weeks were filled with misery. Kyle, who was a student at the nearby University of Virginia, came to see Jacqueline in his new Corvette. His lavish gifts and his promise to buy whatever kind of home Jacqueline wanted even convinced her parents that this young man was such a good catch that she didn't have to wait until she was twenty to marry him.

Having lost Jacqueline, Mark decided to go to South Dakota to see if there really was hidden treasure. He'd show her! He'd show up in a Corvette of his own. She'd be sorry!

But he cleaned out his desk five times and couldn't find the map. No matter. He thought he remembered well enough to go without it. He knew the people who had rented the farm would be happy to let him look over the old family homestead, and no one would notice the garden spade he carried in his backpack.

When he arrived, the people were friendly enough. "Our farm is pretty popular," the farmer's wife told him. "Just three month's ago, a tall blond man driving an old car with Virginia license plates came here with his friends as part of a project with the University of Virginia to dig for Indian artifacts. They think the Sioux Indians lived here for several years."

Suddenly, Mark came to a horrible realization! Kyle Smith must be his cleaning lady's son! His inspection of the area where the gold had been hidden confirmed his suspicion. Because he had neglected one treasure, he had lost another.

THIS WAY OUT →

☑ Asking God to Meet Legitimate Needs

You, like Mark, have the map indicating the location of an incredible treasure—the wisdom that comes from God and His Word! After you have accepted Christ as your Savior, obtaining this wisdom is your greatest need. Then the other things you want—holiness, prosperity, healthy friendships—will be yours as well.

Listen to what wisdom will do for you, as recorded in Proverbs 8:17–21:

> I love those who love me, and those who seek me find me. With me are riches and honor, enduring wealth and prosperity. My fruit is better than fine gold; what I yield surpasses choice silver. I walk in the way of righteousness along the paths of justice, bestowing wealth on those who love me and making their treasuries full.

Dear God, give me your wisdom. Keep reminding me that it's more important than anything else.

✔ Getting the Facts Straight

What you go after with all your heart you usually get. Deciding to search for God's wisdom can change your whole life.

> So I [Jesus] say to you: Ask and it will be given you; seek and you will find; knock and the door will be opened. Which of you fathers, if your son asks for an egg, will give him a scorpion? If you then, though you are evil, know how to give good gifts to your children, how much more will your Father in heaven give the Holy Spirit to those who ask him! (Luke 11:9–13)

> Blessed are they who keep [God's] statutes and seek him with all their heart. They do nothing wrong; they walk in his ways. You have laid down precepts that are to be fully obeyed. (Psalm 119:2–4)

> Your statutes are wonderful; therefore I obey them. The unfolding of your words gives light; it gives understanding to the simple. . . . The statutes you have laid down are righteous; they are fully trustworthy. (Psalm 119:129, 130, 138)

Because of laziness, fascination with the spectacular, and a desire to do our own thinking, we look for shortcuts and new ways to obtain wisdom. There are none. God has ordained that we must constantly search the Scriptures and continually call upon the guidance of the Holy Spirit, with a sense of humility and willingness to submit to God's will.

✔ Rethinking the Situation

Trudy's English teacher only gave her a *B-* on her theme—but she liked it anyway. Maybe it was true that gold could not be kept in the family for five generations and maybe nobody would be as foolish as Mark. But Trudy identified with Mark. She knew she was doing something just as senseless.

She really believed God meant it when He said:

> Blessed is the man who finds wisdom, the man who gains understanding, for she is more profitable than silver and yields better returns than gold. She is more precious than rubies; nothing you desire can compare with her. (Proverbs 3:13–15)

And Trudy knew where to find wisdom. Yet, she read novels by the dozens and watched soap operas on TV, rarely opening her Bible. If she didn't change, maybe she'd wake up someday and find herself married to an atheist or meditating in an Eastern religion, or who knows what. Like Mark, she was neglecting her treasure map and taking great risks.

Finally, she thought of an idea. Her pastor had talked about "accountability partners"—meeting with another Christian on a regular basis to check up on each other spiritually. Since she knew that Candy maintained a steady devotional life, she decided to give her a call. After explaining her situation, Trudy asked if Candy would meet with her each week, because having to report to another person would be a powerful incentive to change her ways. Candy was delighted and said she'd been praying for an "accountability partner."

Together they picked out a devotional book for teens and in addition decided to read a chapter each day in the New Testament. As she read, Trudy prayed for wisdom. After a while, her Bible study replaced her half-hour soap opera. Trudy could tell the difference in her life now that God's thoughts were beginning to crowd out the trash that had been filling her mind.

✔ Putting the Truth Into Practice

Determine that your lifelong goal will be to seek God's wisdom and to cry out for spiritual understanding. Don't be as careless with your hidden treasure map (God's Word and prayer) as Mark was with his—because you don't want to lose out on a great many of God's promises.

CHAPTER 4

The "Class C" Miracle

Amanda had a tendency to be lazy. She loved to eat.

She looked over the size 14's for the darling dress she'd seen in the store window—only to discover that it came only in sizes 6–12. That was the moment she decided to go running every morning *and* to stop eating chocolate.

But at 6:00 A.M. the next day, sleeping-in seemed like a better option.

When her little brother predicted that someday she'd weigh 300 pounds, Amanda joined Weight Watchers. That lasted two weeks. Then she signed up for aerobics with her girlfriends, but only halfheartedly did the exercises. Usually, she convinced the others to stop for ice cream on the way home.

Because they lived near the lake, Amanda then vowed she'd go swimming every day that summer. But a few days after school let out, she opted for a new hairstyle, which made swimming too much of a hassle.

Then on the youth retreat Amanda met Josh. They found they had a lot in common: a genuine desire to serve Christ, love for fun, fondness for spectator sports, and plans to study chemistry in college.

After dating for a while, Josh confided, "I like you a lot, but there are two things that really bother me—your laziness and your addiction to food. I'm really concerned that you'll ruin your health and your self-image."

Amanda realized the seriousness of her problem. She saw that her bad habits might be a stumbling block to her non-Christian friends and could even drive Josh away. Although they were only high school seniors, she really loved Josh and was beginning to think that someday she might even marry him. But maybe he didn't want a wife who kept gaining weight and was too lazy to do her share of the work. She was ready to make a lifelong commitment to conquering gluttony and laziness.

"You say you believe in miracles," Josh went on, "but you don't really believe that God can help you lose weight and make you into a person who enjoys hard work. If you confess your sinful attitudes and cooperate with Him, He'll begin to work in you. I'll do my part. We can go running together and we won't go out for ice cream anymore."

And Amanda *did* change. Every day she prayed that she'd recognize the self centered desires which plagued her, and she asked for strength to act as God directed. She rejoined the aerobics class her girlfriends were taking and put her heart into the exercises. She kept praying, "Jesus, I love you and I'm doing this for you." She started to enjoy running with Josh. Whenever she wanted brownies and rocky-road ice cream, she placed her focus on her greater goal—doing God's will.

The day came when Amanda put on a new size 10 dress for a very special date with Josh. To most people this was only a "class C" miracle, but to Amanda it was a supernatural demonstration of the power of God.

THIS WAY OUT

☑ Asking God to Meet Legitimate Needs

Amanda didn't realize the absolute necessity of a lifelong exercise and weight control program until Josh laid it out on the line. Maybe you're equally unaware of the commitment you must make to search out God's wisdom and His will as revealed in the Bible. Perhaps you're unaware of how a little disobedience can spoil cherished hopes and plans.

No one would deny that accepting Christ, like falling in love, is a neat emotional experience. But for the long-haul relationship, day in and day out, through good times and trials, through broken romances and award assemblies, through chemistry experiments and missed free throws, you must depend on knowing God's will and doing it. Love is based on action. God showed His love for you by sending Jesus to die for you and to freely forgive *all* your sins. You say "I love you too" by obeying His commandments.

Dear God, give me a hunger for your Word and a desire to express my love to you through obedience. Help me realize how serious the consequences of straying from you really are.

☑ Getting the Facts Straight

1. Your love relationship with Jesus is based on finding out what God wants you to do and then doing it. Jesus said, "If anyone loves me, he will obey my teaching. My Father will love him, and we will come to him and make our home with him" (John 14:23).

2. If you have a good love relationship with Jesus, everything else will fall in line. When you put God and His instructions first in your life, you're doing yourself a big favor. "But seek first his kingdom and his righteousness, and all these things will be given to you as well" (Matthew 6:33).

☑ Rethinking the Situation

Some time later, Amanda did marry Josh. As she held their little baby boy in her arms, she realized how good God had been to her. She felt happy and fulfilled. However, she had gained a lot of extra weight during her pregnancy and she dreaded the thought of going on a strict diet to take it off. Now that she didn't go to work anymore, she thought of how nice it would be to sleep in each morning.

But she remembered the words Josh had spoken to her over six years before: "I like you a lot, but there are two things that really bother me—your laziness and your addiction to food. I'm real concerned that you'll ruin your health and your self-image." And in spite of ten rationalizations she could think of off-hand, she knew that her decision to be diligent and get back on a diet would improve both her testimony and her marriage. So she set her alarm for 6:30 A.M. and conquered the desire for a dish of ice cream before she went to bed.

☛ Putting the Truth Into Practice

Besides your main purpose of glorifying God in all you do, make a list of the important goals you have in life. Like becoming an elementary schoolteacher, having a happy marriage, owning a nice home, becoming a youth leader in church. Then explain how failing to follow God's wisdom expressed through His commandments could shatter each of these dreams. (If you don't follow God's rules on diligence, you might not study hard enough to graduate from college. Not obeying God's laws about avoiding sex before marriage could force you to marry someone you don't really love. If you don't take God's advice on finances, your debts might keep you from ever saving up enough money to make a down payment on a house. If you neglect the Bible's teaching on holiness, the church leadership might have to choose someone else to work with the young people.

Like Amanda, you'll face times when a slump *seems* inevitable. But you don't have to fall for Satan's lie. If you continually seek after God's wisdom as if it were pure gold—and it's far more valuable—you'll be richly rewarded.

Goals	*How failing to obey God's commands could destroy my chances*

CHAPTER 5

Great Ideas—And Their Not-So-Great Results

It was hard, but the decision was final. The plant where Jim's father was supervisor was closing in two months and he had to transfer or lose his retirement and all his benefits. Even though it was the middle of Jim's senior year, there was no choice but to move across country to Nashville.

Jim decided to make the best of it. He took his pastor's intensive discipleship course so he'd be ready to be a missionary to his new school.

When he registered at Jefferson High, the counselor carefully looked at his school records. Because of his good grades and high test scores, she suggested he take "Great Ideas," an honors class for students whose grammar and writing skills were already at college level.

Jim enjoyed the challenge and competition in a class full of "brains." They were required to read a book every two weeks—and some of the writers were obviously anti-Christian. Because Jim's views were, as the teacher put it, "a strange combination of outmoded fundamentalism and modern insight," he really had to be on his toes. He became so busy with schoolwork that he hardly had time to open his Bible. Every book he read for "Great Ideas" contradicted what he believed. The teacher and his fellow class members brought up questions he'd never considered. How could he be positive that *everything* in the Bible was true? Was Jesus the *only* way to God? How could he *prove* God existed?

Instead of bringing his questions to an older Christian who'd already investigated the tough intellectual problems, he tried to think things through for himself. Instead of studying the Bible more and letting God give him answers, he decided to delve into every philosophy on his teacher's recommended reading list. He made friends with some of the guys in his class, and soon began to think a lot more like they did.

THIS WAY OUT

Asking God to Meet Legitimate Needs

God wants to give you answers to your questions. When Thomas doubted, Jesus didn't bawl him out. He showed him His hands and His side.

Dear God, show me what the truth really is. I've been wondering about _____. Lead me to a good Christian who can give me an answer. Open your Word to me more fully.

Getting the Facts Straight

1. If you don't hang on to the truth and constantly review it, you'll lose it.

My son, do not forget my teaching, but keep my commands in your heart. . . . Let love and faithfulness never leave you; bind them around your neck, write them on the tablet of your heart. (Proverbs 3:1, 3)

My son, keep my words and store up my commands within you. Keep my commands and you will live; guard my teachings as the apple of your eye. (Proverbs 7:1, 2)

Buy the truth and do not sell it. (Proverbs 23:23)

You must constantly read, study, memorize and meditate on God's Word or you won't be able to stand up against the bombardment of falsehood and error from media, textbooks and casual conversation.

2. If doubts creep in, *don't panic*. The enemies of Christianity have been trying to destroy it for twenty centuries. It's highly unlikely that someone you know is going to come up with a completely new "contradiction" capable of discrediting faith in Christ! Even if some new discovery seems to threaten your faith, remember that "science is a train that is always moving." Some of the things that were "scientific facts" a hundred years ago seem ridiculous today. Wait until all the evidence is in.

Jesus said it best: "Heaven and earth will pass away, but my words will never pass away" (Matthew 24:35). God's Word has always stood the test of time, and it always will.

✍ Rethinking the Situation

Jim decided it would be better to believe in a universal consciousness than in a "slaughter-house religion." It seemed more lofty to see God in everything than to believe in a God who demanded a blood sacrifice for personal sin. And he dumped the idea of hell, figuring that reincarnation gave everyone lots of chances—it just took some people longer than others. His parents thought he was going out for debate, but really he went to meditation classes with his teacher and the best students from the "Great Ideas" class.

Although Jim wasn't a very faithful church attender in Nashville, he did go to the Sunday morning service with his family when they returned to the old hometown for vacation. There was a guest speaker, a Christian university professor.

"It's dangerous to make up *your* idea of God," he emphasized, "because the inventor is always greater than the thing invented. All man-made religions put their emphasis on what man does.

"Every religion on earth, except for biblical Christianity, tells you that there is something you can *do* to get to Heaven or Paradise or Nirvana. They refuse to believe that Jesus shed His blood on the cross to pay for your redemption. And they all minimize or disregard the Bible. They change it, misinterpret it, add other sacred writings, or replace it with visions and mystical experiences. Many of these spiritual experiences are real, but the person sees and talks with demons, not with God."

Jim shuddered. If the "ascended masters" his teacher talked about were really demons, he'd better get out before it was too late. After a long talk with the guest speaker, he confessed the sin of making up his own religion, invoking the name of a Hindu god in his meditation class, and opening himself to demonic forces. He thanked Jesus for dying for him, and dedicated his life to God.

✍ Putting the Truth Into Practice

Don't ever stop reading your Bible. Even if you don't feel like it, even if you have doubts. Even if you don't think you're getting anything out of it. Seek answers from sincere Christians who have studied the intellectual questions facing Christianity. If your pastor can't help you, make an appointment to talk about your questions with another. Discuss your doubts with a Christian college professor. Go to a Christian bookstore and ask for a book that will address some of your questions. Write letters to Christian experts in the field.

But most of all trust God to give you His answers.

CHAPTER 6

The Graduation of the Goddess

Brittany frantically looked through her books and notebooks in search of her English theme. Desperate, she began to clean out her locker. Suddenly it dawned on her. She'd left the folder that contained her composition on the dashboard of her father's car, and he had driven off that morning for two days of sales meetings in Boston. "I'm such a dummy!" she scolded herself out loud. "Nobody else would do something so idiotic."

"You mustn't say that," her friend Katie interrupted. "You're a good person and you have a divine nature. It's just that you haven't learned to recognize the god inside you. You just need to have your thinking altered so you can overcome your sense of inferiority and understand that you're part of the divine consciousness. That means that whatever is possible for God is possible for you. I'm learning how to meditate just right so I'll realize my great potential. That's what you need to do."

Brittany had always been taught that she was a sinner and couldn't save herself. But she had to admit that there was something attractive about the idea that she had the ability to realize her own godhood. If it was just a matter of learning the correct method, she could work hard and achieve the goal. The whole concept appealed to her. Maybe someday she'd graduate as a goddess.

☛ Asking God to Meet Legitimate Needs

You need to be free from the condemnation of the devil. He constantly tries to accuse you. He attempts to make you feel guilty for sins that have already been forgiven. He tries to blast you for being human, for not having a perfect memory, not being able to do every-

40

thing right the first time, or not being as intelligent or as talented as your friend. Accept the fact that you're human and you make mistakes.

Then learn to live in Jesus, confessing and forsaking each sin, sensing the freedom that forgiveness brings.

Dear God, show me what "therefore, there is now no condemnation for those who are in Christ Jesus" means for me. I'll confess sin but I won't accept fake guilt trips the devil tries to lay on me. Teach me to discern the difference.

✔ Getting the Facts Straight

1. *You are human, not divine.*

As a father has compassion on his children, so the Lord has compassion on those who fear him; for he knows how we are formed, he remembers that we are dust. (Psalm 103:13, 14)

God is in heaven and you are on earth, so let your words be few. (Ecclesiastes 5:2)

There is a great difference between the Creator and us, His created ones. The desire to be like God caused Eve to commit the first sin. Pretending to be what you are *not* also causes great strain. Accept the limitations of being human *and* the supernatural resources God gives to those who depend completely on Him.

2. *You are a sinner who cannot save yourself—but you can be forgiven.*

For all have sinned and fall short of the glory of God. (Romans 3:23)

If we claim to be without sin, we deceive ourselves and the truth is not in us. If we confess our sins, he is faithful and just and will forgive us our sins and purify us from all unrighteousness. (1 John 1:8, 9)

Sinners are not worthless—it's just that they need Jesus—the Sin Eradicator. God made you unique and special. No one can duplicate the beauty of your personality, your creativity, and your abilities. But God created you to be dependent on Him for every breath of air, for every step you take, and for your eternal salvation. Living in accordance with your Designer's plan will result in a great deal of freedom and enjoyment.

3. *Wisdom comes from God, not from inside you.*

And if you call out for insight and cry aloud for understanding, and if you look for it as silver and search for it as for hidden treasure, then you will understand the fear of the Lord and find the knowledge of God. For the Lord gives wisdom, and from his mouth come knowledge and understanding. (Proverbs 2:3–6)

In order to become wise, you must pray and search the Scriptures. You can't trust your own ideas and those from other human sources.

✔️ Rethinking the Situation

Brittany went to meditation classes with Katie. She did everything the Guru told her to do. After a while, physical existence seemed more and more distant as she increasingly lived in a mystical daze. Soon grades and boys and holding down a job seemed unimportant to her. She was completely lost in her own world.

By obliterating reality, Brittany "listened" to the "god" inside—and that god told her that the establishment was a farce, that competition for grades was bad, and that she was almost divine now in spite of the fact that her relationship with her parents was worse than ever, her grades were terrible, and no one could penetrate the wall she was building up around herself.

Even when she flunked out of school and her parents kicked her out of the house, she never reexamined her ideas. After all, the "god inside" made no mistakes.

✔ Putting the Truth Into Practice

Don't fall into Brittany's deception. Truth is found in God and His Word, not inside *you*. Remember that you are human and therefore you make mistakes. Each day, you must ask God for wisdom, and for His opinion on

how to study
what to do on your dates
how to get along with your parents
how to reform your thought life
how to better organize your time
which friends to choose
how to improve your personality
how to break bad habits
how to be a good worker
which courses to choose and which job to take
how to contribute something positive to your church
which clothes to buy
what music to listen to.

CHAPTER 7

The Choice

Cherie sat down on the couch and paged through *Time* magazine. She was waiting for the doorbell to ring. Troy was an hour late, and that worried her. Their time together was so precious she didn't want to miss a minute of it.

Troy was the kind of guy she'd always dreamed of meeting—intelligent, witty, handsome, always thoughtful and sensitive. She'd suggested that he come early for their dates so they could talk *before* they went out instead of after. They were getting serious and Cherie wanted to avoid the temptation of getting too physical.

"I appreciate that you have such high standards," Troy had said at the time. "You help me obey God." Cherie was in love, and she knew that guys like Troy were hard to find.

When she heard him drive up, her heart skipped a beat.

After a couple of minutes of casual conversation, Cherie asked, "How was the meeting you attended last night?"

Excitement danced in his eyes as he explained to her what he'd experienced at the "Spirit/Mind Control" seminar at the local community center. "I learned how to be controlled totally by the Spirit. They taught me how to blank out my own thoughts, will, and emotions so that everything that passed through my mind would be from God. I never thought 'walking in the Spirit' could be so easy."

"Wait a minute," Cherie interrupted. "The devil could also put thoughts into your mind. We need to check out all our ideas and actions with the Word of God."

Troy reassured her. "If our motives are right, we can't be deceived. Christians have discernment that keeps them from being misled."

"Troy," Cherie agonized, "do these people you met with last night believe that the Bible is the Word of God?"

"Sure they do," Troy countered. "Don't you trust my judgment? Do you think I'm some kind of heretic or something?"

"Of course not," Cherie soothed. "But we have to be careful. There are a lot of cults out there, and they can look pretty good at first."

"Well, next Thursday night I'm going again," Troy said firmly. "If you'd like to come, fine. If not, I'm going anyway."

Cherie panicked. Losing Troy was the thing she feared most in the whole world. But something inside told her that this new group Troy had told her about was very dangerous for spiritual health.

THIS WAY OUT

☛ Asking God to Meet Legitimate Needs

Some *easy formula* for having all supernatural knowledge is *not* a legitimate need—even if it sounds appealing. The apostle Paul exclaimed, "Oh, the depth of the riches of the wisdom and knowledge of God! How unsearchable his judgments and his paths beyond tracing out!" (Romans 11:33). Your real need is to trust in the God who knows everything and has given His commandments to promote your well-being. Cling to God and everything He says in His Word instead of falling for some deceptive shortcut.

Dear God, thank you that I can trust you whether or not I understand everything. Keep me from embracing some system that makes faith unnecessary. Make me diligent in my Bible study and guard me from any idea that would tell me that something new has replaced searching the Scriptures.

Getting the Facts Straight

There is *always* a problem when someone claims to have a new revelation or method that is not *specifically* stated in the Bible and was not practiced by the New Testament church. Any group that claims to understand everything is dangerous. God is greater than we are, and certain things will always be a mystery. Deuteronomy 29:29 tells us: "The secret things belong to the Lord our God, but the things revealed belong to us and our children forever, that we may follow all the words of this law." God in His knowledge has shown us the things we really need to know. Other things remain mysteries, perhaps so we will have to trust Him more.

God could have chosen to impart His wisdom through audible verbal instruction, or through an inner voice straight from heaven to everyone sitting in lotus position. He didn't.

Instead, He gave us His written Word and commanded us to search the Scriptures for wisdom. Whenever anyone offers a "spiritual life" that basically bypasses the serious study of the Bible, something is drastically wrong. Jesus said, "If you want to enter life, obey the commandments" (Matthew 19:17). True spirituality, apart from studying and applying the Bible to your life, does not exist.

It is *not* true that if your motives are pure, you'll never be deceived. Many people are sincerely wrong. Only the truth found in God's Word can guard us from error. The Bible tells us to review God's Word, constantly studying, understanding and obeying it.

Do not add to what I command you and do not subtract from it, but keep the commands of the Lord your God that I give you. (Deuteronomy 4:2)

These commandments that I give you today are to be upon your hearts. Impress them on your children. Talk about them when you sit at home and when you walk along the road, when you lie down and when you get up. Tie them as symbols on your hands and bind them on your foreheads. Write them on the doorframes of your houses and on your gates. (Deuteronomy 6:6–9)

My son, keep my words and store up my commands within you. . . . Bind them on your fingers; write them on the tablet of your heart. (Proverbs 7:1–3)

How can a young man keep his way pure? By living according to your word. I seek you with all my heart: do not let me stray from your commands. I have hidden your word in my heart that I might not sin against you. (Psalm 119:9–11)

✓ Rethinking the Situation

Because of the war raging in her heart, Cherie spent a sleepless night. One part of her wanted to stick with Troy no matter what he did. But her deeper desire, which finally won out, was to put Jesus first regardless of the cost.

The next day she called her pastor and asked if she could see him. When she gave him the name of the group Troy had visited, her pastor shook his head and commented, "That group is a cult, and they're really off-base." Then he explained their whole doctrine to Cherie, telling her why she had to stay clear of them.

Cherie drove home and then went to her room and sobbed. It was the hardest thing she'd ever done, but she told God that if she had to choose between Him and Troy, she'd choose Him. Then she called Troy to try to convince him to talk to her pastor.

"Cherie," he said with finality, "I received direct enlightenment on Thursday night. I discovered the way to live the Christian life without effort. If you don't believe me and the whole group, I guess there's no point in seeing each other any more."

After she hung up the phone, Cherie cried and cried. But deep down inside a peace also began. She knew she'd made the right choice.

✓ Putting the Truth Into Practice

Humbly accept the word planted in you, which can save you. Do not merely listen to the word, and so deceive yourselves. Do what it says. Anyone who listens to the word but does not do what it says is like a man who looks at his face in a mirror and, after looking at himself, goes away and immediately forgets what he looks like. But the man who looks intently into the perfect law that gives freedom, and continues to do this, not forgetting what he has heard, but doing it—he will be blessed in what he does. (James 1:21–25)

Decide to continually study and obey everything in Scripture. Stay far away from any group that replaces Bible study with meditation, or chanting, or new revelation, or mystic practices.

CHAPTER 8

Is It Right?

"This exercise," explained Miss White, Carrie's social studies teacher, "is designed to help you discover your own value system.

"Shakespeare said it hundreds of years ago, 'To thine own self be true.' Most of you have been squeezed into molds by your parents, your churches, and society at large. But *you* are important. You're the captain of your own soul. You have the ability to make your own decisions about what's right and wrong.

"For example, my parents taught me never to lie. But, I can think of several situations in which lying would be the kindest and most humane thing to do. Maybe your parents taught you that sex outside of marriage just isn't worth it. And for those who carry a heavy guilt complex, it isn't. But maybe you're different. Maybe it's right for you. Some say that robbing is always bad, but stealing food makes a lot more sense than starving to death. People have such diverse personalities and needs that what's correct for one person might not suit the needs of another."

Carrie had never thought of things that way before. She'd always believed that some things were right and some things were wrong—*period*. But her teacher's philosophy did seem logical. Maybe it was true that she was the only one who could decide what was right for her.

☞ Asking God to Meet Legitimate Needs

Don't equate your value with the "right" to decide what sin is "for you." You weren't created to decide what's right and wrong any more than you were created to fly. That in no way reflects on your worthwhile personality, your unique talents or your intelligence. God built

49

right and wrong into the universe, and you can't ignore that without paying the consequences. "In all your ways acknowledge him, and he

THIS WAY OUT

will make your paths straight" (Proverbs 3:6) is solid advice. A mother who really loves her child refuses to let him make his own decisions on whether knives, matches and broken glass make good playthings. Likewise, God cares about you too much not to warn you about lying, stealing, sex outside of marriage, and pride.

Dear God, give me a true sense of self-worth based on my relationship with you. Thanks for making the standards of right and wrong. Help me to always obey you.

🖊 Getting the Facts Straight

If you want any machine or gadget to work well, you follow the manufacturer's instructions. The designer who made it knows what it can do and how it will work best. In the same way, your Creator knows how you will be happiest and most fulfilled. The Bible is full of promises for those who live by His rules.

All these blessings will come upon you and accompany you if you obey the Lord your God. (Deuteronomy 28:2)

✒ Rethinking the Situation

Carrie was watching a national TV program. The host announced that his next guest would prove that fact was stranger than fiction.

A good-looking young man told about being trapped in an elevator with a crazed gunman who said he'd shoot anyone who believed in Jesus. When the gunman questioned the young man about his beliefs, he had replied, "I believe that Jesus is the Son of God. He's my personal Savior. In the name of Jesus, you drop that gun." To the amazement of everyone the gunman started shaking and put down his pistol. When the elevator door opened, two policemen were waiting there to make the arrest!

After interviewing two of the eye-witnesses, the TV host returned to the young man. "Why did you tell the truth?"

"I don't believe in situational ethics," he replied. "What's right is always right, and what's wrong is always wrong. I live by God's standards that are found in the Bible. If God weren't all-powerful, and if He couldn't work miracles, people might be able to say that sometimes it might be necessary to lie or steal or cheat. But if I were starving, I wouldn't rob a bakery. I'd pray. The God I serve fed a whole nation for forty years in a barren desert. I'm sure that He'd feed me."

"Do you boss God around in your prayers?" the interviewer wanted to know.

"No way," the young man answered. "God is God. If He chose not to do a miracle to save me, I'd be content to die for the truth and go to heaven. My attitude is the same as the three Jewish dudes in Daniel's day who refused to worship idols. They said, 'If we're thrown into the blazing furnace, the God we serve is able to save us from it. But even if he doesn't, we will not serve your gods or worship the image of gold you've set up.' " (See Daniel 3:17, 18.)

Carrie wondered if Miss White was watching the same program. She realized that she'd forgotten how big God really is. She had just assumed that she was left to fend for herself. Now Carrie could see that if she obeyed God, the Creator of the universe could take care of her without her little lie or petty theft.

✒ Putting the Truth Into Practice

Make Proverbs 3:7 your motto: "Do not be wise in your own eyes; fear the Lord and shun evil." Determine in your heart that God's Word is the only guide for right and wrong.

Make a list of things that the Bible says are wrong even though most people consider them acceptable. Alongside each one, write out a verse which clearly states that the action is sinful. (If you don't know your Bible very well, get someone to help you.)

Things That Are Wrong   *Bible Verse That Proves It*

_____   _____
_____   _____
_____   _____
_____   _____
_____   _____

CHAPTER 9

Drifting, Dreaming, and Dashing Against the Rocks

One of the things Bruce liked most was to take his new little sailboat out on the lake. Drifting along, watching the clouds above, made him feel as if reality and responsibility were a thousand miles away. The only problem was that drifting and dreaming basically characterized his life.

Sitting in English class, Bruce was not about to hear Mrs. Martinson bawl out the class and threaten to flunk anyone who didn't turn in a term paper on time. Instead, he thought of what it would be like to go sailing in the Mediterranean . . .

Mentally, he was just passing the French Riviera when the teacher walked up to his desk and demanded to see his research cards and what he had written so far. Bruce blinked out of his daydream and handed over a pack of empty note cards and a couple sheets of paper with an introduction and a few ideas.

"Young man, do you expect this to evolve into a term paper in just two weeks?" demanded Mrs. Martinson. Everybody laughed.

When the grammar lesson began, Bruce drifted off to the Riviera again.

But there were things that penetrated Bruce's fantasy shell: determined teachers like Mrs. Martinson, confrontations with his parents, tongue-lashings from his sister when she got fed up with doing more than her share of work around the house.

One day Dick met Bruce in the hall before school. "Why don't you forget about classes and skip school with us today? Who needs six hours of boredom?"

Since this was the day his nonexistent term paper was due, Bruce gladly accepted. About ten guys sneaked out and went to Dick's house. They smoked pot, played cards and watched TV. Although Bruce had never been high before, he liked the feeling.

He began smoking pot regularly. Doing drugs made him oblivious to the rude intrusions of reality. Because he was high, the ugly scene that came when his parents received his fail notices hardly affected him.

Bruce absorbed the life philosophy of a friend and decided that he could create his own reality. His goal became escaping the "evil physical world" by exercising his mental powers which he believed became expanded through the use of drugs and through meditation.

THIS WAY OUT →

📝 Asking God to Meet Legitimate Needs

Escaping the reality of daily living is *not* one of your basic needs. Jesus, the Son of God, left heaven to come and live on earth as a man, who needed to eat and sleep and work in a carpenter's shop.

Proverbs is full of advice on dealing with personal relationships, managing money, guarding your tongue, living successfully in this work-a-day world. What's necessary is learning to obey God *here* and *now*—sensing Jesus' presence and strength as you board the school bus, order hamburgers, call your girlfriend and take drivers' training.

True Christianity is about overcoming, not escaping. It's about conquering, not running; miracles, not manufacturing masks to hide behind.

Dear God, thank you that you are willing to give me all the power I need to live a victorious Christian life in the middle of sarcasm, Satanism, selfishness, and stomachaches. Help me to remember that through you I am more than a conqueror. Thank you for putting the treasure of yourself in a jar of clay like me.

✔️ Getting the Facts Straight

A discerning man keeps wisdom in view, but a fool's eyes wander to the ends of the earth. (Proverbs 17:24)

The lips of the righteous nourish many, but fools die for lack of judgment. (Proverbs 10:21)

Folly delights a man who lacks judgment, but a man of understanding keeps a straight course. (Proverbs 15:21)

A fool denies reality. But if we are set on obeying God, we'll face the here and now and we'll do our work well.

Men and women of God have always been very much involved in the real world. Paul gave his fellow travelers some common-sense advice, Dorcas made clothes for needy children, the early church took care of widows, and Jesus himself washed the disciples' feet. If you read the biographies of great Christians such as Hudson Taylor, George Mueller, D. L. Moody, and many others, you'll find that they were diligent in all the details of daily living. If you want to count for God, you'll finish your homework, answer your mail, straighten up the house, wash the car, and take out the garbage.

✔️ Rethinking the Situation

Blotting out reality didn't bring the happiness Bruce wanted. He began to combine drugs, which produced some bad trips. There was also a gnawing fear that he was falling under the control of some evil force.

Then he saw a poster announcing that an ex-drug addict was appearing at the auditorium on Saturday night, giving a talk on "I Found Something Better." He decided to go.

The man explained that drugs had driven him to the point of nearly killing another man in a fight. And he couldn't remember what he'd done. Some savage force had taken control of him.

"After I accepted Christ," the man said, "my life changed completely. But I'd divorced myself from reality for so long that I had to take special steps to renew my mind. I chose a factory job, where I'd have to concentrate on doing my work as fast and as accurately as possible. I memorized Scripture and took Bible courses. The road to recovery wasn't easy. But it was completely worth it."

When he asked those who wanted Jesus to change their lives to come forward, Bruce responded. He prayed for forgiveness and invited Jesus to take control of his life, and felt as if he'd stepped from the foggy night into the bright sunlight.

☞ Putting the Truth Into Practice

Do you escape into your daydreams? Do you try to sidestep reality? Have you had the habit of getting high or taking tranquilizers whenever things got tough? Probably everyone would have to answer yes to one of these questions. The cure is discovering the power you have in Christ—knowing that in Jesus you have the resources to squarely face up to the situation. Memorize and meditate often on the following verses:

> I can do everything through him who gives me strength. (Philippians 4:13)

> He replied, "I saw Satan fall like lightning from heaven. I have given you authority to trample on snakes and scorpions, and to overcome all the power of the enemy; nothing will harm you. (Luke 10:18, 19)

> No, in all these things we are more than conquerors through him who loved us. (Romans 8:37)

> You dear children are from God and have overcome them, because the one who is in you is greater than the one who is in the world. (1 John 4:4)

CHAPTER 10

And What About Tomorrow?

Lance lived his life by the minute. He couldn't be bothered with planning for the future. He never cracked a book unless there was a test. Because he was a "brain," he could get decent grades just by last-minute cramming. His spur-of-the-moment decisions drove his mother nuts. She had to cancel the surprise birthday party she'd been planning for him because instead of going to the store to buy ice cream for his mom, he drove to his brother's home in another city. He'd spend his money like water, and was usually penniless three days after getting a paycheck.

The same attitude carried over into spiritual matters. He figured he was young so he could have his fling and repent later. What mattered most to him was having a good time *now.*

One beautiful day in early spring, Aaron rode up on his motorcycle. Lance enthusiastically accepted the invitation to go for a ride and jumped on his own. Although there were still a few icy patches on the road, Aaron said, "How 'bout a race."

After a long winter, that sounded good to Lance.

He gunned it.

The sensation of speed was awesome. The wind felt good in his face. He looked back, satisfied that he was well ahead of Aaron.

An instant later he skidded on a patch of ice and lost control. There was a crash, indescribable pain. Then nothing but blackness.

☑ Asking God to Meet Legitimate Needs

It is important that you avoid the foolishness of living for the moment without considering the future. Part of wisdom is making long-range plans and weighing what effect present actions will have in the years ahead.

Dear God, teach me to examine each action and to live with eternity's values in view. Help me to make wise plans so I can have an enjoyable future.

THIS WAY OUT →

Getting the Facts Straight

> Understanding is a fountain of life to those who have it, but folly brings punishment to fools. (Proverbs 16:22)

What you build into your character as a young person affects your whole life. Therefore, Satan spends incredible time and energy propagating the lie that the young need to live it up and sow some wild oats. The myth that you can decide to settle down any day you choose without reaping what you've sown has ruined many lives. Foolishness brings its own punishment. Poor work habits, the things you never bothered to learn in school, addiction to junk food, or always blowing your budget will come back to haunt you.

> The path of life leads upward for the wise to keep him from going down to the grave. (Proverbs 15:24)

Most people don't plan for their eternal future—and that's part of the whole satanic strategy which the book of Proverbs calls foolishness. Fatalism says, "I just live for today and hope for the best. Tomorrow will bring what tomorrow has." Living like this is not only foolish, but it keeps you from your best achievement—and from going to heaven.

✍ Rethinking the Situation

Through a fog of pain and heavy medication, Lance fought to return to consciousness—vaguely aware that he was in a hospital. Although he couldn't open his eyes or move, he heard his mother greeting his dad. "I'm so glad you got on the early plane. I just can't go through this alone."

Concentration proved too much effort and Lance slipped into oblivion. When he came to again, he heard his parents praying out loud. Somehow he knew he'd make it.

During the months of recovery, Lance was forced to face the future. If he wasn't willing to do painful exercises now, he might never walk again. He had to do special reports and a tremendous amount of homework or face failing the year. Because of his live-for-the-moment spirit he'd come very close to waking up in hell, and he never wanted to run that risk again.

Lance surrendered his whole life to Jesus. He'd had enough of foolishness and was ready to begin his search for wisdom.

✍ Putting the Truth Into Practice

Don't let your life just happen. Take time to plan with God. Remember, "Plans fail for lack of counsel, but with many advisors they succeed" (Proverbs 15:22).

1. Write out your long-range goals. (Like, A. Win others for Christ; B. Study my Bible more; C. Stand up for what's right; D. Go to college; E. Marry the person God has for me, or remain single if that is God's special plan for my life.)

2. List the things you must do *this week* to help make these goals

a reality. (Like, A. Take Barbie/Bobby for a Coke and present Christ *to him or her*; B. Read through Philippians in one sitting; C. Be respectful to Mr. White even though no one else is; D. Study hard for the geometry test in spite of the fact that I dislike math; E. Do my work around the house cheerfully and well as preparation to be a better husband or wife.)

Long-range Goals	*This Week's Contribution to Fulfilling Them*

CHAPTER 11

The Beginning of Success

Mara was angry and bitter. Being seventeen and married was a real downer. And she hated being pregnant. Although she didn't have morning sickness anymore, she felt tired, ugly, and uncomfortable.

She'd always been a top student and now she had to try to keep up her grades—and their apartment. Learning to cook was harder than she thought it would be. Instead of the church wedding she'd always dreamed of, there had been a simple ceremony in the pastor's home. A weekend in the city was their honeymoon, because they had to be in school on Monday morning. And although Gary treated her okay, she was beginning to see how immature he really was. Also, his mother was paying their bills—and running their lives.

Gary wasn't accustomed to picking up after himself, so this morning he'd left clothes all over the bedroom floor, homework all over the front room, and everything he'd taken out to prepare a bag lunch on the kitchen counter. He'd kissed her a quick goodbye and gone off to play baseball and spend Saturday with the guys.

As usual, she was left alone. She felt out of place with her girlfriends, so there was nothing for her to do. Besides, Gary's mother had always waited on him hand and foot and he expected Mara to do the same. That meant an immaculate house, meals on time, clean clothes, and a lot of work.

As she vacuumed, she couldn't help thinking of her messed up dreams.

If it hadn't been for all the problems connected with her pregnancy and getting married, Mara would have been the valedictorian of her class. In spite of everything, she still held on to second place. But being eight months pregnant, she didn't look forward to stepping out onto the platform to receive her award. She'd planned to go away to college. With a baby that would be impossible. Although Gary was a nice guy, he wasn't the kind of man she would have married if things had worked out differently. He'd most likely settle down in Colombia as an auto mechanic. She might as well give up her dreams of traveling to Europe, attending great concerts, and directing outstanding choirs—unless someday she got a divorce and met somebody new.

Where was God? Why had He let her fall in love with Gary? Sure, they'd had sex outside of marriage, but so had dozens of other couples in their high school. She could name at least ten girls in the senior class who'd played with the same fire, but they'd be attending the graduation dinner in trim tight-waisted dresses. She'd used contraceptives and been "responsible." Why did God let *her* get pregnant? It just wasn't fair.

Asking God to Meet Legitimate Needs

You have to recognize that God makes the rules. He promises blessing for those who live by them and cursing for those who break them. (Read Deuteronomy 28.)

When you break God's laws, you must confess your sin and realign your life with biblical principles in order to receive the blessing again.

*Dear God, I acknowledge that I broke your rule when I
_____. It's my fault. I ask for forgiveness and won't*

repeat my wrong action. Thanks for your pardon and for restoring to me "the joy of your salvation."

☞ Getting the Facts Straight

A man's own folly ruins his life, yet his heart rages against the Lord. (Proverbs 19:3)

The integrity of the upright guides them, but the unfaithful are destroyed by their duplicity. (Proverbs 11:3)

Blaming God and other people for *our* sins started with Adam, and it's never stopped. Adam didn't confess, "Yes, I ate some of the forbidden fruit and it's all my fault." Instead, he defended himself with, "The woman *you* put here with me—*she* gave me some of the fruit from the tree and I ate it." When you're sure that God should have run His universe differently, watch out. Being on the verge of wanting to be God yourself is very dangerous—that was Satan's big sin.

There is a way of handling every situation *without* blaming God. By putting this information into practice, you'll experience God's constant blessing in your life:

1. When you break God's laws, remember that you deserve the consequences. But when you agree with God that you've sinned and that your punishment is just—when you stop your wrongdoing, God can turn even your mistakes into blessings. For example, an unwed mother can learn to trust God to help her raise her child and to work in her life to the point that she'll be a testimony to many others. God can make her life meaningful and beautiful. It's the person who maintains that he or she is right and God is wrong who suffers a whole lifetime for one sin.

2. When something bad happens to you *which is not your fault,* your responsibility is to maintain a scriptural attitude. If you apply a "we-know-that-in-all-things-God-works-for-the-good-of-those-who-love-Him" mentality, you'll come out on top. If you blame God, you'll suffer needlessly. Someone has said, "Sorrow either makes you bitter or better."

I once heard a teenage girl who was raped give a radiant testimony of God's grace and victory in her life.

In a Christian bookstore I met a lady whose face shown with the love of Jesus. Although I'd never seen her before, I was drawn to that happy countenance. When I began to talk with her, I learned that she had lost her husband and all her children in an automobile accident.

God can make you an overcomer in any circumstance.

Some things are very deep and very traumatic, though, and you may need the help of a Christian counselor to deal with feelings that lie beneath the surface. But blaming God will never help you.

3. Because as a Christian you have authority over the forces of evil, you are not a victim. When you call on the name of Jesus, you receive power.

A girlfriend of mine was walking alone at night. A thief grabbed her purse. She screamed, "In the name of Jesus, you give that back to me!" He dropped it and ran.

Three missionaries sat in a hut surrounded by drunken cannibals. The missionaries prayed and prayed. About 2:00 A.M. everyone left. Years later after many of these Africans were converted, one man asked the missionary, "Where did you get the army that came to guard you the first night you spent here with us?" The astonished missionaries replied, "There was no army. God must have sent His angels!"

If you have to live with the consequences of your own sin or that of others, pray for strength and victory and you'll receive it. Prayer changes things like tragedy, trauma and handicaps. Best of all, prayer changes you. Because it's the presence, the love and the miraculous touch of Jesus that transforms the bad into the beautiful, we must always stick close to Him and be connected to His power.

☑ Rethinking the Situation

Instead of finishing cleaning the apartment, Mara sat down and cried. When the telephone rang, she tried to compose herself enough to answer. But she didn't fool Tera, who was on the other end of the line. "I just called to see how you were doing," Tera explained. "You sound kinda down. Do you mind if I come over?"

"Please come," Mara answered, still sniffling. When she hung up, she tried to straighten up the apartment a little before Tera arrived. *It's funny,* thought Mara. *Tera is the only friend I have who would never sleep with her boyfriend, and she's been the most caring and supportive.*

Tera brought tuna fish sandwiches and Cup-a-Soup so they could have lunch together. As they talked, Mara told her exactly how she felt. Tera listened attentively and then began to share. "Mara, your problem is that your moral standard is different from God's. God says that sex outside of marriage is wrong—period. It doesn't matter if everyone is doing it. Regardless of what you've been taught, there's no way to sin 'responsibly.'

"If you want to get out of this rut, you can! Agree with God that you've sinned—not only in this area but in many others—and that you need a Savior. You can accept Jesus and the forgiveness He offers. If you give yourself completely to Him, your life and your marriage can be transformed. God can take what you think is second best and make it into something wonderful."

Mara did ask Jesus to come into her life and to forgive all her sins. It seemed strange to her, but she could sense that admitting failure was the beginning of success.

▶ Putting the Truth Into Practice

It's foolish to blame God, or others. Turn off the voice that says, "If only I'd had different parents, or grown up in a different neighborhood, or had Fred's brains or Lily's looks." The touch of the artist makes the masterpiece —not the material from which it's made.

1. Squarely face your sin without trying to make excuses. God, I confess _____ (whatever sin you committed). It's *my* fault, and I confess it to you.

2. Check your attitudes. List the problems you have because of circumstances or the sins of others. Confess any wrong attitudes. After each one, write out all the words of Romans 8:28 and how you'd react if you *completely believed* that verse.

3. Daily pray in faith for *strength* and *victory* and *God's viewpoint* on each situation.

CHAPTER 12

Are You a Slave to "Curiosity"?

Barry invited Ian over to his house after school so they could work on their project for the science fair. When Ian saw all the pictures on Barry's bulletin board and a stack of *Pin-Up Magazine*s, he let out a gasp of surprise.

"Ian, are you still an 'innocent little boy'?" Barry mocked. "I can lend you a couple of copies of *Pin-Up*."

"I don't know," Ian stammered. "I've never read stuff like that before."

"What *century* are you living in, man?" Barry jeered at him. "Get with it."

Not wanting to risk more ridicule, Ian carefully hid two copies in his notebook.

When he got home he stashed the magazines in his bedroom. After supper, he helped his dad clean out the garage, finished his homework and then got ready for bed. Setting the alarm clock, he crawled into bed and turned off the light. But as he lay there in the darkness, he was overcome by a wave of curiosity. What was he missing out on, anyway?

Ian switched on the light and dug out a copy of *Pin-Up Magazine*. After staring at the centerfold, he started reading one of the articles. It said that "purity" was outdated and sexual activity was necessary for health and virility. Ian had never heard such a thing but wondered if it might be true.

The other articles and pictures were even more shocking. He had a hard time calming down his emotions in order to get to sleep.

The next day at school he kept mentally undressing the girls and envisioning them in the centerfold of *Pin-Up Magazine*. All he seemed to be able to think about was sex.

Although he knew it was wrong, he hurried home from school and read everything else in the magazine. One article told him that girls liked having sex with the guys they dated, and if one became pregnant it was her own choice since she could have taken steps to prevent it. Another affirmed that someone in Paris had already discovered a cure for AIDS, but that it had not been made public because of a conspiracy of the governments to try to control the sexual habits of their people. At first he wondered, but then he thought, "If it's in print, it must be true."

Ian was getting hooked fast. He borrowed more magazines from Barry and even bought some of his own. His thought life changed drastically, but he convinced himself that he was just a normal, red-blooded teenage boy.

THIS WAY OUT

☞ Asking God to Meet Legitimate Needs

A basic necessity for your health and happiness is holy living, which includes a clean thought life. If you have questions about sex, direct them to a mature Christian who can give you correct answers. The devil is out to destroy every young person, and he'll use every lie and deception available to pollute your mind and drive you into sexual sin. Be smart enough to resist.

Dear God, help! I'm having a hard time controlling my thoughts. Show me how to keep my mind so full of your Word that there is

no room for trash. Keep me from falling into Satan's sex trap.
Thank you that you've got the power and that it's available to me.

◤ Getting the Facts Straight

Stay away from a foolish man, for you will not find knowledge on his lips. The wisdom of the prudent is to give thought to their ways, but the folly of fools is deception. Fools mock at making amends for sin, but good will is found among the upright. (Proverbs 14:7–9)

A wise man fears the Lord and shuns evil, but a fool is hotheaded and reckless. (Proverbs 14:16)

A fool finds pleasure in evil conduct, but a man of understanding delights in wisdom. (Proverbs 10:23)

The wicked freely strut about when what is vile is honored among men. (Psalm 12:8)

The fool decides that sin and its consequences don't exist. He is reckless and deceived. Furthermore, he enjoys doing what's wrong. When there are a lot of fools around "what is vile is honored among men."

For example, today, because most people think illicit sex is okay, no one bothers to check the validity of the studies, reports and "scientific" findings that uphold it. Even laws such as abortion upon demand support wrong actions. This is an age in which wrong is worshiped, so the guilty go free, facts are distorted and what's right is ridiculed.

The basic foundation on which foolishness is built is the idea that sin and its consequences do not exist. It's in the classroom, in the media and sometimes in the church. A line of reasoning, like a wall, becomes completely faulty if it's built on a crooked footing. Christians should learn everything they can, study hard, go to college and take courses—but they should always be aware that every branch of learning built on the proposition that sin is okay or nonexistent will be wrought with problems. Foundations for foolish thinking include:

1. Each individual is free to express himself or herself sexually in any form they desire without answering to anyone.
2. There is no God, and therefore there's no right or wrong and no reason for existence. Everything living sprang from inanimate forces that evolved over millions of years, finally producing human beings.
3. Everything is relative and there is no absolute truth. Right and

wrong depend on the century, the circumstances and the society.

4. Man is the measure of all things. The human being is practically a god, capable of making the world better and solving all his own problems.

Watch out for "research" that is designed to support one of these or other false theories. *Nothing that is truly wise will contradict God's Word.*

Rethinking the Situation

When Ian arrived home from school, he found his mother sitting at the kitchen table with her head resting on her arms. She was sobbing. He rushed to comfort her. "Mom, what's the matter?" he asked sympathetically. "Did something happen to Grandma?" She only cried harder.

Finally, she moved her arm slightly, revealing a copy of *Pin-Up Magazine.*

Ian gasped. Not knowing what to say or do, he went to his room. An eternity of guilt and condemnation followed. It was 7:00 P.M., and still there'd been no call to supper. He figured his parents were having a summit meeting.

Then his dad entered his room. "I need to have a talk with you," he ventured. "Your mother and I have known for a long time that something was wrong. You just haven't been yourself. Now that we know what the problem is, we can deal with it.

"I looked over your magazines. What I saw made me sick to my stomach. They're not only perverted, they contain the biggest bunch of lies I've ever read. Any doctor could tell you that the junk printed in that magazine is pure fiction."

"I'm sorry," Ian volunteered. "Barry made fun of me, and I guess I just got curious. But once I started reading that stuff, I became addicted. How can I get this junk out of my mind?"

"First," his dad suggested, "you must confess your sin to God and get rid of all your pornographic material. Then we'll work together on memorizing Scripture. You know that I was twenty-two before I accepted Christ and that I didn't come from a Christian background. I had a lot of trouble with impure thoughts. When I took a Scripture memory course, it really made a difference in my thought life. It's a matter of stuffing your mind so full of the right things that there's no room for the bad. I'm sure it will also work for you."

✔ Putting the Truth Into Practice

Memorize these verses:

> For with you is the fountain of life: in your light we see light. (Psalm 36:9)

> The fear of the Lord is the beginning of knowledge, but fools despise wisdom and discipline. (Proverbs 1:7)

> Let God be true, and every man a liar. (Romans 3:4)

Remember these verses when you're tempted to say, "The Bible says 'such-and-such,' but modern studies prove otherwise."

CHAPTER 13

Your Own Worst Enemy: Self-defense

Laura's mother died when she was five. A year later, her father remarried. The year she entered junior high, things really got tough.

One night she woke up and realized that her father and stepmother were having an argument.

"I don't want your girls in the house," her stepmother was saying. "Send them to your mother. I've never seen two more maladjusted girls in my life. Besides, they don't like me. Now that we have our own baby, I don't want him to have to compete with his half sisters for your attention."

"But you promised to be a mother to my girls before I married you," her father protested. "I want my girls with me, and I love them. It's a package deal," he said with finality. "Me *and* my daughters, or we're through."

Laura's stepmother never mentioned the topic again, but when their father wasn't around, she took out her bitterness on Laura and her sister. Laura was told that she was ugly and dumb. Her stepmother constantly complained that Laura worked too slowly, that she was forgetful, and that she did a poor job of baby-sitting her little brother.

Laura developed a strategy for dealing with all this verbal abuse: she became defensive. If her stepmother said she did a poor job of cleaning the kitchen, her instant reply was, "No, I didn't." If her history teacher complained that she wrote her report without doing enough research, her machine-gun reply automatically went off. When her father cautioned her about wearing her clothes too tight and her skirts too short, she flared, "I'm not going to put on the stuff girls wore twenty-five years ago when you were young!" She never stopped to consider the facts before giving her defensive response.

One afternoon she was walking home from school wearing the tight sweater and the super short skirt that had touched off an argument between her and her father at breakfast. A handsome man in a sports car drove up alongside her. "I've been watching you," he confided. "My name's Tom—and you're beautiful. You're the kind of girl I'd like to spend my money on. Let me give you a ride home."

THIS WAY OUT

They drove around town, and as he dropped her off, Tom arranged to pick her up that evening to take her to one of the fanciest restaurants in town.

Laura never told anyone where she was going. And when she got home that night, her father was waiting up for her.

"Laura," he confronted her, "I don't like the looks of that man one bit. He's got to be thirty, and you're still a teenager. I'm forbidding you to see him."

"I'm *sixteen*, and I'll run my own life, *thank you!*" snipped Laura as she hurried upstairs to her room.

She did continue to see Tom, secretly. He treated Laura respectfully, bought her gorgeous clothes and jewelry, and took her to expensive places. She impressed girls at school with her reports about their dates.

On Valentine's Day, Laura admired herself in the mirror. Tom had given her an elegant red velvet dress. He'd also reserved front row seats at the opera. This sure beat going with some high school punk to a basketball game. She was glad she was running her own life.

After their midnight dinner, Tom reached into the glove compartment, took several small bags and laid them on the front seat. "Laura," he said firmly, "your dress has secret pockets in the lining. Put these bags in the pockets and hide them in your room until I need them."

"What's in the bags?" Laura asked.

"Cocaine," answered Tom.

☞ Asking God to Meet Legitimate Needs

Maybe you, like Laura, have served as a scapegoat for someone else's frustration. Perhaps you've suffered verbal abuse and unjust treatment. It's essential that you open up and allow Jesus to heal the hurts of the past, and that you abandon your "nobody's-gonna-tell-me-what-to-do" defense system.

Dear God, you know that I'm defensive and I have a hard time accepting advice. Heal my past wounds and show me how to receive constructive criticism.

☞ Getting the Facts Straight

Do not speak to a fool, for he will scorn the wisdom of your words. (Proverbs 23:9)

A fool finds no pleasure in understanding but delights in airing his own opinions. (Proverbs 18:2)

A whip for the horse, a halter for the donkey, and a rod for the backs of fools! (Proverbs 26:3)

Though you grind a fool in a mortar, grinding him like grain with a pestle, you will not remove his folly from him. (Proverbs 27:22)

A foolish son brings grief to his father and bitterness to the one who bore him. (Proverbs 17:25)

He who trusts in himself is a fool, but he who walks in wisdom is kept safe. (Proverbs 28:26)

A fool is so stubborn that he or she won't change. All advice and attempts to produce reasonable reactions are futile. A fool likes his or her ideas so much that he or she would rather repeat them over and over than hear anything new or anything wise. Because a fool often hurts others, it is sometimes necessary to inflict physical pain or discomfort to stop him in his tracks. Reasoning would do no good. The parents of the fool suffer not only the disappointment of seeing a child make a bad decision, but the constant agony of watching a person who will not change repeat the same errors over and over.

Because the person who refuses to change or admit wrongdoing is a prime candidate for hell, the devil does everything possible to cultivate the kind of soil in which such foolishness can grow. He'll use every bit of injustice, betrayal, cruelty and neglect to create an atmosphere of fear and suspicion. Then he'll tell you that God is dead, or impersonal, or that He just doesn't care and you're alone in the world, so you don't dare to trust anyone but yourself. He'll convince you that you'd better build high walls of self-defense so nothing unpleasant can penetrate.

The cure for refusing to change your mind is this: Line up your thoughts with God's, and you'll receive so much security from the fact that God loves you unconditionally that admitting you're wrong is no longer threatening. Whenever you don't agree with God, you're wrong. And He often uses other people to point out your faults.

Rethinking the Situation

When Laura got home that night, she was panic-stricken. Staring into the darkness in her room, she imagined herself surrounded by drug dealers and men from the mafia. Maybe her phone was bugged. Maybe she was being followed.

Somehow, the thought that none of this would have happened if she had listened to her father passed through the thick barricade she'd built around her conscience. A year before, Laura's stepmother had accepted Christ as her Savior and changed completely. She'd even apologized to Laura for all the awful things she'd said, and she tried to do everything to make it up to her. But Laura remained unmoved. She would allow nothing to melt her bitterness.

The darkness became unendurable, and Laura turned on the light. On her dresser, amid the clutter, she spied a plate of homemade fudge and a tract entitled, "Penetrating the Wall of Self-defense."

She began munching and reading:

"It doesn't matter how you got started with your 'my-mind's-made-up-don't-confuse-me-with-the-facts' mentality. For some people, self-defense is so ingrained you can't even suggest that a little exercise would do them good, or that parking a yard from the curb on a narrow street is less that brilliant, or that mailing a letter without a stamp might not be advisable. The person who *will not* change is asking for trouble.

"The first step in removing your defense system is deciding to trust God instead of yourself. Surrender every opinion to Him. He won't make fun of you. He won't deceive you. He won't disappoint you. What He says is absolutely true.

"Second, you must realize that your self-worth stems from the fact that Jesus loved you enough to die for you—not from proving that you're right. There's no limit to what God can do through you if you'll only surrender to Him completely."

Laura was sobbing. She cried out to God, "Lord, I admit I'm wrong. I've been very foolish. I want *you* to run my life and make my decisions. Come into my heart right now and forgive me for everything I've done to offend you."

The peace and relief she felt was so great she almost forgot about the problem she faced. Instead of relying on her own insight, she'd admit to her parents that she'd been wrong—for a long time. She would ask for their advice and help.

▶ Putting the Truth Into Practice

Although your problem may not be nearly as serious as Laura's, most of us have built up some defensiveness. Ask God to show you when you rationalize wrong behavior and refuse to accept correction. It could also be helpful if you asked your parents and a couple of close friends to point out areas of defensiveness they see in you. Change comes only after squarely facing facts.

1. Make a list of areas in which you rationalize. (Like making excuses for not going on a diet, for not studying, for not keeping things in order, for not obeying your parents.)

2. Cross out each excuse and write out the truth. Then pray to God who works miracles and ask Him to help you be an overcomer in that area, to accept good advice, and to form new habits.

CHAPTER 14

Falling for a Fool

For three days, Bernie had studied for the big biology test. She hardly cared what grade she got anymore; she just wanted it to be over. The class filed in more silently than usual and she tried to keep from biting her fingernails.

Mr. Boyer stood by his desk. As soon as the bell rang, he made his announcement. "I'm sorry, but I wasn't able to type up the test last night. My little girl became extremely ill and we had to rush her to the hospital. We'll have the exam on Monday instead."

Jay rose to his feet. "It's not fair!" he shouted. "We're all psyched for the test *now*. You've just ruined my weekend. You tell us to plan ahead. If *I* gave you some excuse like that and asked to take the test another day, you wouldn't let me. When *we* have to stay home because of emergencies, you give us a harder make-up test. You're nothing but a hypocrite! I'm going to the office to protest. Who wants to come along?" Because Mr. Boyer had canceled tests before, made frequent excuses for not handing back homework on time, and had lost some of their big projects, several students walked out with Jay.

Bernie remained seated, but she felt a lot of sympathy for Jay. He was so handsome and fearless. Maybe he went too far, but she knew he was going hunting this weekend and wouldn't have time to study.

When she saw him at lunch, she asked, "How'd it go?"

"We didn't get anywhere," he admitted. "Principals are paid to stick up for teachers. Students have no rights." Jay enjoyed having someone listen sympathetically to his complaints and invited Bernie to eat with him. Somehow to Bernie, Jay seemed like a misunderstood kid who'd do fine if only someone like her would believe in him.

The following day, Bernie listened to Jay's Newman-the-Nerd routine as he made fun of his gym teacher.

Just then Shane walked by.

"Teacher's pet!" sneered Jay. "You don't have a brain in your head, but Newman-the-Nerd gives you straight *A*'s because you lift weights."

"I got an *A* on the exam," Shane shot back, "and I have perfect attendance. You deserve to flunk! The only muscle you have is in your mouth."

At that, Jay was on his feet—and his fist missed Shane's face only because he ducked. The lunchroom supervisor was there in a flash and ordered Jay to the principal's office. Knowing that the supervisor wasn't allowed to leave his post and that the school policeman had just left the building, Jay refused and sat down to finish his meal.

"Jay," Bernie suggested kindly, "it would be better for you to go to the principal's office voluntarily. If you don't, your punishment will be even worse."

"I thought you had more sense than that," Jay derided her. "You're just a dumb blond who thinks students should be pushed around. Don't tell me what to do, okay?"

Tears filled Bernie's eyes.

"And don't you start slobbering," Jay warned, "or people will think I hit you."

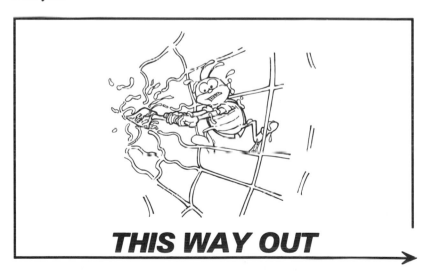

THIS WAY OUT ➡

☑ Asking God to Meet Legitimate Needs

Saying anything you want and acting just as you please is *not* something you need. These things characterize a fool. True happiness comes from permitting Jesus to work inside you to remove all the seething lava of hate and bitterness that could erupt into anti-social behavior.

> *Dear God, please take away my resentment against authority. I admit I'm still angry because of* _____. *Clean it all out. Thank you, Lord, that you can transform those emotions which could cause me to act like a fool. You can turn hate into love, bitterness into forgiveness, envy into self-acceptance, and revenge into caring. I allow you to work that kind of miracle in my life.*

☑ Getting the Facts Straight

A fool shows his annoyance at once, but a prudent man overlooks an insult. (Proverbs 12:16)

Stone is heavy and sand a burden, but provocation by a fool is heavier than both. (Proverbs 27:3)

Mockers stir up a city, but wise men turn away anger. (Proverbs 29:8)

If a wise man goes to court with a fool, the fool rages and scoffs, and there is no peace. (Proverbs 29:9)

A fool gives full vent to his anger, but a wise man keeps himself under control. (Proverbs 29:11)

But wisdom that comes from heaven is first of all pure; then peace loving, considerate, submissive, full of mercy and good fruit, impartial, and sincere. (James 3:17)

Very seldom do you meet someone who is one hundred percent a fool. But if a person displays too many of these foolish symptoms too often, you are well-advised to stay away. A wise man and a fool cannot talk things over because the fool can do nothing but show anger and ridicule others. Reasoning with a fool is impossible. Thinking that the totally foolish person can be helped by your love and understanding leads to disappointment. Only God can change a fool.

Unfortunately, none of us is above displaying *some* of these foolish characteristics. And we'll never stamp out these defects unless we treat them like sin, repent and receive God's grace to live differently.

Don't say, "Oh, I have a quick temper, that's all." Admit, "Just like a fool I showed my annoyance at once." Don't use the excuse, "Oh,

I was just upset." Confess that if you had been wise, you would have turned away anger. If you fly off the handle or make fun of another, treat it as a serious offense—against God and the person you hurt.

▶ Rethinking the Situation

Jay got suspended for three days, and Bernie walked to his house every day after school to bring him his homework assignments. He robbed the refrigerator while she did his homework for him.

When Jay returned to school, Ms. Bremmer (who, according to Jay, was the world's most unreasonable English teacher) became the topic of lunch conversation. Jay showed Bernie the assignment sheet giving the requirements for the three book reports due by March 15. Jay asked Bernie for help—and that meant Bernie would do them all.

One day, Jay and Ms. Bremmer had an ugly scene in the classroom. Jay was determined to get revenge. He knew that she lived alone and decided to scare her with some frightening phone calls. When he told Bernie, she protested. Snatching the last completed book report from her hands, Jay stormed off, vowing to find a girlfriend who really understood him.

The next day, he was eating lunch with Vicki.

At last Bernie realized that she'd fallen for a fool.

▶ Putting the Truth Into Practice

Seeing a fool in full bloom should make you afraid of turning out like that. Now is the time to eradicate your foolish characteristics. When do you show your annoyance at once? (In a traffic jam? When someone insults you? When Aunt Bertha calls you "darling"?)

When do you provoke others? (By carrying your teasing too far? Name-calling? By ridicule? By procrastination?)

When do you stir up others? (By spreading gossip? By organizing the revolution against an unfair teacher? Starting a food fight in the lunchroom?)

Make a "Working for Wisdom" chart. Every time you resist the temptation to do one of the foolish things listed, give yourself a star—maybe even a treat!

Working for Wisdom			
Blowing up when someone insults you.			
Ridiculing someone until they get angry.			
Arguing with someone just to make yourself look good.			
Getting angry before getting the facts.			
Refusing to obey your parents until they get upset.			
Spreading gossip.			
Putting down a person in authority.			
Taking revenge on someone who has wronged you.			
Stirring up anger and rebellion in others.			
Putting off responsibilities that affect others.			

CHAPTER 15

Wise Up

Sure, Michael loved Jesus and wanted to follow Him. He hoped his life would count for something. But he felt he had too many strikes against him. Too much to overcome. His mom was an alcoholic—and a prostitute who lived on welfare. He had no idea who his father was. Besides, he'd been hit by a car while playing in the street as a child, and the injury had left him permanently handicapped.

He had accepted Jesus as his Savior at a Christian camp for underprivileged children. But even among the poor, he felt like the bottom of the barrel. And though the people at the church he attended showed him love and concern, he felt out of place. They dressed nicer than he did. The boys were all excited about the church basketball team and, of course, he couldn't play. Other kids did things with their families, but he had nobody.

Evan, for example, had everything. Wonderful Christian parents, money, brains, athletic ability, looks and musical talent. To Michael it seemed that God could have at least divided it between them fifty-fifty.

One day he read a verse in the Bible: "A wise servant will rule over a disgraceful son, and will share the inheritance as one of the brothers" (Proverbs 17:2). In that passage he saw a very important principle—the key to rising above his background and circumstances was to obtain God's wisdom.

He thought of his favorite Bible character, Joseph. Being sold as a slave was worse than the situation in which Michael found himself. Even then, Joseph kept seeking God's wisdom. The day came when he ruled over all of Egypt. He got the job because, as Pharaoh noticed, "there is not one so discerning and wise as you."

All Michael knew was that the "fear of the Lord is the beginning of wisdom." So he decided that seriously studying and applying everything he found in the Bible would give him wisdom.

As he put diligence into practice, his grades improved and he was offered a high-paying part-time job working with computers. Realizing the absolute necessity of forgiving, he fully pardoned his mother, and his deep bitterness toward her gradually disappeared. One day she even went to church with Michael, and there she gave her life to Jesus. Their home was transformed.

Michael saw that there was always more of God's wisdom to learn. He had only scratched the surface, but already his life had changed for the better. His number-one goal became knowing God and His wisdom.

☑ Asking God to Meet Legitimate Needs

Dear God, keep me from assuming that I'm wise. Help me to see that YOUR wisdom is the way out of my problems and my impossibilities. Give me a great hunger for divine insight. Make me diligent in looking for it each day as I search the Scriptures. Teach me to apply your wisdom to every area of my life.

☑ Getting the Facts Straight

A wise man has great power, and a man of knowledge increases strength. (Proverbs 24:5)

A fool's talk brings a rod to his back, but the lips of the wise protect them. (Proverbs 14:3)

A king delights in a wise servant, but a shameful servant incurs his wrath. (Proverbs 14:35)

A man is praised according to his wisdom, but men with warped minds are despised. (Proverbs 12:8)

A wise man attacks the city of the mighty and pulls down the stronghold in which they trust. (Proverbs 21:22)

God's wisdom gives power and protection—it was dangerous to mess with Daniel because the Lord takes care of those who follow Him. As you receive God's wisdom, you'll sense His strength and strategy for dismantling the devil's strongholds in your life and in the world around you. Finally, the person who's filled with God's wisdom demands respect. When the Queen of Sheba visited Solomon, she was super impressed.

✔ Rethinking the Situation

Ten years later, Michael was happily married and held down a good job. Because he'd worked so hard for what he had, he appreciated it all the more. And he never stopped enthusiastically studying God's Word to store up more wisdom. He *planned* to give his children the things he never had, but even more important he wanted them to acquire a deep hunger for the wisdom of God.

One day as he left his office, Michael noticed a man about his age on the street. He was rather poorly dressed and obviously high on something. And he looked strangely familiar. A second glance gave him a start! It looked like Evan. It couldn't be—but it was!

Stopping to talk, Michael discovered that Evan had thrown his faith overboard and now believed that God was the invention of man's mind. His wife had left him and he had no steady job. But he was so lost in his philosophical ideas that he didn't seem to notice that anything was wrong.

As he drove home that night, Michael thought of the times he'd wished he could change places with Evan. Now he was totally thankful to be himself. And he realized the terrible danger of substituting human "wisdom" for the knowledge that comes from God.

✒ Putting Truth Into Practice

Most people are so certain of their own wisdom that they minimize God's promises. They decide that wisdom doesn't bring prosperity, because they are having financial problems. Since they lack strength, they don't really believe that wisdom and power go together.

It's better to admit that maybe you're not so wise than to change God's Word. Gaining God's wisdom takes a lifetime of readjusting your life to conform to it.

1. Rewrite Proverbs, chapter 2, in your own words.

2. List three specific things *you* must do to really search for wisdom.

Self-Examination

Part I: The Wise Man and the Foolish Man

1. In order to put God's rules for daily living into practice, you must

_____ a. fall in love with Jesus and get to know Him better and better;

_____ b. realize that breaking any of God's commandments brings serious consequences;

_____ c. believe that obeying God brings His blessing;

_____ d. trust God for the power to do the right thing.

2. What excuses have you been giving for neglecting the treasure map of God's Word? _____

_____

_____

What changes do you plan to make in order to search out God's wisdom? _____

_____

_____

3. What should you do when intellectual doubts about biblical Christianity plague you?

_____ a. Panic.

_____ b. Interview a mature Christian who has studied these questions.

_____ c. Wait in faith for the "new discovery" that seems to disprove the Bible to be refuted.

_____ d. Study the Bible more thoroughly, and pray for God's answers.

4. Which ideas are true?

_____ a. You should listen to "the god within."

_____ b. You're a valuable person who's completely dependent on God for breath and forgiveness and salvation.

_____ c. Wisdom comes only from God, not from within you.

_____ d. If our motives are right, we can't be deceived.

5. "True spirituality apart from s _____ and a_____ the B _____ to your life does not exist."

6. Which of these ideas are false?

_____ a. You're important enough to decide for yourself what is right and what is wrong.

_____ b. Reality is in your mind.

_____ c. You should attempt to escape the nuisances of daily living and ignore your body.

_____ d. You have the ability to live victoriously in very tough situations, because Jesus, who lives within you as a Christian, is greater than any power on earth.

7. List three occasions when you've given in to the foolishness of living for the moment without considering the future. _____

_____

How are you going to avoid the foolishness of rash decisions living with eternity's values in view? _____

_____

8. If you don't want to suffer needlessly, don't b _____
God for the consequences of your sins and the wrongdoing of others.

9. What is the foolish person's idea regarding sin?

_____

_____

10. Which is *not* a step that will lead you out of defensiveness?
    _____ a. Trust God instead of yourself.
    _____ b. Forgive the people who have wronged you and let God heal the hurts that have caused your defensiveness.
    _____ c. Accept your defensiveness since you really can't change.
    _____ d. Realize that your self-worth is determined by the great love Jesus has for you, not by proving you're right.

11. What is the key to rising above your background? _____

_____

_____

---

1. a, b, c, d; 2. Personal; 3. b, c, d; 4. b, c; 5. Studying, Applying, Bible; 6. a, b, c; 7. Personal; 8. Blame; 9. Sin and its consequences do not exist; 10. c; 11. Constantly searching out God's wisdom as found in the Bible and applying it to your life.

Part Two

Love and Friendship

CHAPTER 16

The Real Roxanne

Moving from a farm in Kansas to San Diego had been very hard on Rick. He felt totally out of it—a country hick, a Midwest misfit. Back in Centerville High he'd been president of Future Farmers of America, a basketball star, and an honors student. His father's death and his mother's remarriage to a wealthy San Diego businessman had changed everything. The new Corvette, the expensive clothes and the generous allowance his stepfather provided failed to compensate for his losses.

Rick decided to concentrate on his grades. The prospect of studying at Kansas State University with some of his old friends was the only thing that kept him going—that is, until Roxanne came on the scene.

Beautiful and extremely well-built, she wore miniskirts and tight sweaters. When she strolled up to the English teacher's desk to be admitted as a new student, every eye in the room was on her—and Rick could not get his thoughts back to nominative clauses. This new girl was really something!

Although she flirted with everyone, she singled out Rick for special attention. "You're so handsome," she cooed. "I just love your Kansas accent."

Rick especially enjoyed the jealous glances of the other guys as he walked down the hall with Roxanne. "I'm dying to go to that rock concert Saturday night," Roxanne coaxed as they stopped to view a poster advertisement. "Will you take me?" Rick wasn't even sure it was the kind of music he wanted to listen to and he knew Roxanne wasn't the kind of girl a Christian guy should date. But he said yes, and shelled out $30 a ticket.

When he picked her up on Saturday night, he wasn't quite prepared for her skimpy outfit. "I think you should bring a sweater," he suggested. "You're going to freeze to death."

"Oh no, I won't," she replied. "Just loosen up a little. Relax." Obviously, Roxanne hadn't learned the same first-date etiquette he had. But he thought that going to an ice cream parlor after the concert might keep things calm.

She had other ideas.

After the concert, she begged him to take her to a "favorite spot." They wound up on a deserted beach, where Roxanne began to move in on Rick—real fast.

Rick knew he had to make a decision, and make it quick.

📌 Asking God to Meet Legitimate Needs

You were born with a desire for love and affirmation. If you're desperate for attention, having sex might seem like a solution. But God can fully meet your need for love. The only Person who can constantly understand you and unconditionally love you, no matter what you've done, is God. Learn to sit in His presence and receive His love.

Read the story of the crucifixion, and thank Jesus for loving you enough to die for you. Study the description of heaven in Revelation 7:9–12, 21, 22. Praise the Lord for preparing such a wonderful place just for you. Feel His forgiveness, His presence, His acceptance and His joy.

Personalize this verse: "Let the beloved of the Lord rest secure in him, for he shields him all day long and the one the Lord loves rests between his shoulders" (Deuteronomy 33:12).

Dear God, thank you for loving me. Thank you that there is nothing I can do to make you stop loving me. Thank you that you accept me just the way I am. When I'm tempted to fall for the first available boyfriend/girlfriend—even though I know I shouldn't date that kind of person—remind me of your unfailing love. I receive the security you have for me, and I promise to spend the time with you necessary to develop an intimate relationship.

📖 Getting the Facts Straight

This description of a prostitute in Proverbs fits both guys and girls who will try to tempt you to lower your moral standards. Know what to look for and be on your guard.

> For the lips of an adulteress drip honey, and her speech is smoother than oil; but in the end she is bitter as gall, sharp as a doubled-edged sword. Her feet go down to death, her steps lead straight to the grave. She gives no thought to the way of life; her paths are crooked, but she knows it not. (Proverbs 5:3–6)

Beware of flattery. Test the person's sincerity. Does he or she use compliments as a form of manipulation?

Also, does this person think through decisions? Does he or she weigh the consequences before acting? The immoral person thinks only of momentary pleasures, never of long-range problems.

Is this person incredibly good at rationalizing his or her behavior? Can he or she make wrong sound right? The immoral person sets his or her own standards. God's commandments are not taken literally.

📖 Rethinking the Situation

Six years later, Rick stood at the altar and watched Marcy start up the aisle in her gorgeous wedding gown. She was not only beautiful, but had all the qualities he'd always wanted in a wife. Above all, she was a committed Christian who had kept herself pure just for him.

His mind went back to that night on the lonely beach with Roxanne. His decision to say no had preserved him for this day. Roxanne had told the whole school what happened and a lot of guys made fun of him.

But today, that seemed like something of no consequence. Following God's standard of morality was now paying big dividends—he could give himself completely to Marcy with no regrets.

Marcy and her father had reached the front of the church. As he looked into her sparkling eyes and took her arm, he silently thanked God that he could live this day unmarred by past sin.

☑ Putting the Truth Into Practice

Decide that anyone you date must pass the "Proverbs Test." Make your own list of character traits that are unacceptable after studying the following passages: Proverbs 2:16–19; Proverbs 5:1–14; Proverbs 6:20–29; Proverbs 7:1–27; Proverbs 9:13–18.

CHAPTER 17

How Can So Many People Be So Wrong?

It was a sultry summer afternoon, and Erica was thoroughly bored. Her mom was at work, and the busy signal she kept getting when she tried to call Janie indicated that she was talking to Monica— and that could easily mean a two-hour wait.

She flipped on the TV only to hear a talk-show host making fun of what he termed the "virtuous Victorian lady" who, according to him, was boring, bitter and blue. He contrasted her with today's woman who is dazzling, daring and dangerous. He insinuated that purity belonged to the past when people were unenlightened and uninformed about birth-control methods.

Erica turned off the TV and picked up one of her mother's magazines. The feature article was entitled "Sex Is a Basic Need." It went on to list all the psychological problems you could have if you don't express either your heterosexuality or homosexuality. So this was the kind of stuff her mother read! Her mom had a lot of boyfriends, and although they never discussed it Erica suspected that her mom had affairs with quite a few men.

Six months before, Erica had accepted Jesus as her Savior. She'd gone to club meetings and teen Bible studies where she'd been taught that sex outside of marriage is sin and that it would spoil the beautiful plan God had for her life. Because it was in the Bible, she'd believed it, but now she wondered. How could so many people be wrong? How could the small group of Christians at her school be so sure they were the only ones who were right?

☑ Asking God to Meet Legitimate Needs

The basic need you have is for love, not sex. If sex automatically fulfilled a person, then professional prostitutes would be the world's best-adjusted people and marriage would be the solution to every problem. Although sex is a beautiful expression of love within marriage, used wrongly it causes complicated problems and deep emotional hurt.

THIS WAY OUT →

During your teen years God wants to meet your love requirement through himself and many different people. So often, the young person who falls into sexual sin is the lonely teenager who has no close friends of his or her own sex. Close friendships are God-ordained, and healthy Christian relationships with both guys and girls can keep you from being so starved for attention that you easily fall into any trap.

A friend loves at all times. (Proverbs 17:17)

There is a friend who sticks closer than a brother. (Proverbs 18:24)

And the pleasantness of one's friend springs from his earnest counsel. (Proverbs 27:9)

Dear God, you know I need love and acceptance. You also know how that need can best be met in my life at this time. Send good Christian friends into my life and, if it's your will at this time, a Christian to date.

📓 Getting the Facts Straight

The book of Proverbs equates sexual sin with lack of wisdom. Deciding to search out God's commands and obey them builds in a young person the discernment needed to "flee youthful lusts." Proverbs 22:14 states:

> The mouth of an adulteress is a deep pit; he who is under the Lord's wrath will fall into it.

This verse teaches a principle: The person who falls into sexual sin has already started to disobey God in some other areas.

Proverbs goes to great lengths to expose the stupidity of sexual sin:

> But a man who commits adultery lacks judgment; whoever does so destroys himself. Blows and disgrace are his lot, and his shame will never be wiped away. (Proverbs 6:32, 33)

Because the God who created us loves us, He made rules for our happiness. "It is God's will that you should be holy: that you should avoid sexual immorality" (1 Thessalonians 4:3). This is *the* reason for guarding your purity. However, the fruit of immorality—V.D., AIDS, illegitimate children, abortion, inability to trust a marriage partner and untold heartache should make a person think twice before entering an illicit relationship. Proverbs maintains and experience proves that the immoral person has lost his ability to reason. Whenever we substitute our standards and way of thinking for God's truth, we fall prey to the devil's scheme for destroying our lives.

☞ Rethinking the Situation

Because there was nothing better to do, Erica spent an inordinate amount of time fixing her hair and putting on makeup to go to work. She looked as sharp as anybody could in a drugstore uniform. Since the pharmacy was close to the university campus, she enjoyed attracting the attention of some of the college guys.

But it was the slowest night Erica could remember. She'd spent two hours fixing her hair just for a few ladies and a grandfatherly looking gentleman who was nearly blind!

Shortly before closing time, however, Alex came up to the counter to buy a tube of toothpaste. "Why don't I wait around and take you out for pizza after you get off from work?" he suggested.

"Sounds good to me," Erica returned. "To tell the truth, I'm starved."

They enjoyed each other's company and began dating a lot.

Erica's Christian friends warned her about dating a nonbeliever, but she didn't want to sit home all the time. Alex impressed her with his philosophical ideas and his travels. Besides, she was physically attracted to him.

One night he told her how much he loved her and how beautiful she was. Then he explained that it was time for her to realize her true womanhood. He affirmed that without sexual experience her femininity wouldn't blossom as it should. She seriously considered it—most of a sleepless night.

A couple days later, she left the house early so she could take a walk through the lush green campus before reporting for work. Well ahead of her, walking in the same direction, she saw Alex.

From across the mall another guy called out to him: "Congratulations on becoming a father again! Are you going to send flowers?"

"No," he replied nonchalantly. "I found a girl I like better, and I don't want to give Linda any encouragement." With that he walked on as if nothing had happened.

Erica was stunned. She'd come so close to being his next victim. How could she have believed his nonsense for even a minute? Now she knew her Christian friends were right. And in her heart she prayed, *"Thank you, God, for saving me from my own foolishness."*

✔ Putting the Truth Into Practice

Decide that you'll find out what God's rules are and love His law. Determine that *nothing* but the truth in God's Word will be your moral guide. Memorize these verses:

> You shall not commit adultery. (Exodus 20:14)

> Flee from sexual immorality. All other sins a man commits are outside his body, but he who sins sexually sins against his own body. Do you not know that your body is a temple of the Holy Spirit, who is in you, whom you have received from God? You are not your own; you were bought at a price. Therefore honor God with your body. (1 Corinthians 6:18–20)

Let God fill your need for love and acceptance through the people He will send your way.

CHAPTER 18

Shadows of Shelly

Greg went to church because it was expected of him. He talked like a Christian and (basically) acted like one. But he thought that people who said Jesus was everything to them were just hypocrites. Those young people who were all excited about Bible study seemed a little weird to him. At school he worked hard at being seen as "one of the guys."

When the physics teacher arranged his students in alphabetical order, he was pleased to be seated next to the most beautiful blond in class. Mr. Murphy was out the last two weeks of September, and their do-nothing substitute usually permitted the students to talk the whole hour. Greg took full advantage and finally asked Shelly for a date.

Soon they were seeing a lot of each other. Greg decided that he was falling in love. He thought about Shelly all day long. He dreamed about her at night. And he wanted to be with her constantly. They began to express their affection more and more intimately. Shelly didn't have the standards maintained by Christian girls Greg knew. She did nothing to curb his passion.

They began having sex on a regular basis. Greg did feel guilty, but Shelly seemed to think of it as part of dating—and she had dated a lot of guys before.

One night she told him she was pregnant. When she realized how upset he was, she laid it on the line matter-of-factly. "Either we get married, or I have an abortion. It's your choice."

Greg took a quick mental trip into the future. What would he tell his parents and the people at church? What would happen to his dream of becoming a doctor? How could he face graduation day with an obviously pregnant wife by his side? Shelly had been around and she was fun to date; but he wanted a different kind of wife—one with modesty and loyalty.

Greg chose to break up with Shelly. And she got rid of the baby.

THIS WAY OUT →

☛ Asking God to Meet Legitimate Needs

Dear God, I ask you to keep me pure. Psalm 119:9 tells me; "How can a young man keep his way pure? By living according to your word." Lord, with your help I'll pay attention to everything in Scripture and put it into practice.

☛ Getting the Facts Straight

God's rules prohibiting sex outside of marriage are designed so that you can enjoy the maximum in sexual pleasure—at the *right* time, with the *right* person. The devil wants to rob your enjoyment and cheat you by giving you a dime now instead of a dollar later. Don't permit him to mar one of the most beautiful things God has created.

Drink water from your own cistern, running water from your own well. Should your springs overflow in the streets, your streams of water in the public squares? Let them be yours alone, never to be shared with strangers. May your fountain be blessed, and may you rejoice in the wife of your youth. A loving doe, a graceful deer—may her breasts satisfy you always, may you ever be captivated by her love. Why be captivated, my son, by an adulteress? Why embrace the bosom of another man's wife? For a man's ways are in full view of the Lord, and he examines all his paths. The evil deeds of the wicked ensnare him; the cords of sin hold him fast. He will die for lack of discipline, led astray by his own great folly. (Proverbs 5:15–23)

In other words, let your wife be the well from which you draw love and sexual satisfaction. One interpretation says the springs and streams are the children you will father. How sad if they should be raised by prostitutes, never knowing their real dad. Rather, let them be yours to enjoy. Find delight in your own wife. Never let your love for her diminish. If you commit adultery, God sees you. You'll be forming your own prison with the chains of your sins. "Yielding to immoral sex means losing control of one's life."[1]

My son, give me your heart and let your eyes keep to my ways, for a prostitute is a deep pit and a wayward wife is a narrow well. (Proverbs 23:26, 27)

◪ Rethinking the Situation

Avoiding girls, Greg went through college with a straight-A average and was accepted into medical school. After watching his mother die of cancer with a triumphant spirit constantly praising God, he realized that he didn't have that kind of personal relationship with Jesus. He surrendered his life totally to Christ. Repenting of his pride, Greg asked forgiveness for all his sins, including having sex with Shelly and being responsible for his baby's death. Then he invited Jesus to come into his life. Everything changed drastically and now *he* was the one making fantastic claims about what Jesus was doing for him.

---

[1]Robert L. Alden, *Proverbs: A Commentary on an Ancient Book of Timeless Advice*, (Grand Rapids: Baker Book House, 1983), 53.

When he was sent to General Hospital as an intern, he met Melody—terrific nurse, super Christian and wonderful person. Their courtship became serious. Six months after announcing their engagement, they were married. Greg loved Melody with all his heart and knew that God had given him a real treasure.

Although he knew God had forgiven him, he was plagued by shadows of Shelly. A seven-year-old blond girl made him think of the baby whose death he had caused.

Then one day he saw Shelly in the grocery store. Melody asked him what was wrong. He knew he had to tell her everything. He couldn't stand it any longer. But what would she think?

Would she continue to trust him? Would he ever be able to forget? How he wished he'd listened to those who had taught him the biblical principle that sex was only for marriage and used wrongly would result in hard-to-erase consequences.

✔ Putting the Truth Into Practice

Renew your commitment to save sex for marriage.

If you have fallen into sexual sin, ask God to forgive you and to repair your tattered emotions. Remember that nothing is impossible with God and He can renew your mind and heal your memories. And don't ever let the devil tell you that now that you've blown it, you might just as well keep on sinning. Jesus makes you new and clean. Stay that way.

Determine to stand against all social pressure, temptations and satanic lies in order to maintain your purity for the marriage partner God has for you.

CHAPTER 19

Now or Never

Because Lincoln was overcrowded, some students from Eisenhower Junior were chosen to attend East High. Eddie's name was on that list, and for him it meant being separated from all his closest friends.

That big high school seemed pretty lonely the first month. But he did enjoy sitting next to Todd in algebra class. Todd was the class clown, but he was intelligent as well as witty. Todd wasn't a Christian, but he was a lot of fun to be with. Todd asked Eddie to eat lunch with him, and so Eddie got to meet his friends—the clean-cut jock type of guys.

At first, Eddie felt out of place. They weren't like his Christian friends from junior high. Their jokes were a little off-color, and they made fun of everyone. Sam gave everybody the questions to Miss MacCarthy's English test at lunch and Lane shared the answers for the pop science quizzes. It was a rule that the group always stuck together and no one told on anyone else.

One day, one of the guys brought a few little frogs. He managed to let them loose in the lasagna pan as he passed through the lunch line behind Ted, who got blamed for it. Although Ted was suspended for a day, Eddie was afraid to tell the truth.

Gradually, the dirty jokes seemed funnier, and getting answers for tests didn't seem so bad. "Never rat on a member of the gang" became like the eleventh commandment.

Eddie was invited to Todd's birthday party. The music that blared from Todd's stereo was from a group Eddie's pastor had warned him against. And the pinups Todd had in his room shocked Eddie. But Eddie didn't say anything to let the group know that he was a Christian and that he didn't like this.

As he spent more and more time at Todd's house, though, the music grew on him. He began to long for that familiar beat. He even bought a couple cassettes for himself, to play when his parents weren't home.

One day Darren invited the guys to his house after school. "I'm getting bored," he announced. "It's time we experiment a little. I've got just the thing. My uncle came for a visit and accidentally left all this cocaine."

Todd noticed the look on Eddie's face. "What's the matter? Are you chicken or something?" he asked.

☑ Asking God to Meet Legitimate Needs

Dear God, your Word says, "Bad company corrupts good character" (1 Corinthians 15:33). When I'm at school, help me to stay away from _____ . When I obey you, I know I can trust you to give me a Christian friend instead.

☑ Getting the Facts Straight

He who walks with the wise grows wise, but a companion of fools suffers harm. (Proverbs 13:20)

The fear of the Lord is the beginning of knowledge. (Proverbs 1:7)

Putting these two verses together, you can see that it is not God's will that your close or intimate friends be non-Christians. Certainly you should not date a non-Christian. Of course you will have casual friends who don't know Christ, but if they are influencing you instead of you influencing them, you must change something. Psalm 1:1 lays it on the line:

> Blessed is the man who does not walk in the counsel of the wicked or stand in the way of sinners or sit in the seat of mockers.

If you are receiving advice directly from non-Christians, you'll suffer for it.

✔ Rethinking the Situation

Eddie knew that it was now or never. He prayed silently—first for forgiveness for compromising his Christian principles, and then for strength to escape from this peer-group pressure cooker.

"I have to leave now," he stammered. Although his knees were so weak he felt like an old man, he struggled to his feet, grabbed his jacket and walked out the door. It seemed that those silent stares penetrated the walls and followed him out into the street.

He headed straight for home and closed the door of his room. There he poured out his heart to God and made an important decision: His best friends from now on would always be Christians. He confided in his parents, and together they prayed for a Christian friend that Eddie could hang around with at school.

The next week at East High wasn't easy. With difficulty Eddie explained to Todd that he was a Christian and that he believed doing drugs, passing answers for exams, and telling dirty jokes were all wrong. He assured Todd that he still wanted to be his friend, but that he just couldn't be a member of the gang. Todd's reply was, "That's too bad. I never would have guessed that you're a 'Jesus Freak.' "

Most of the guys in the group made snide remarks when they saw him.

Eddie felt very lonely—looking around at lunchtime for an empty place, going to the basketball game by himself, and being a left-over when the kids in science class paired up to do projects.

But two months later, a new kid from Portland presented his "admit slip" to the gym teacher. Everybody noticed Steve because he hit a home run the first time up to bat. But he drew even more attention in the locker room. When comments headed toward cesspool level,

Steve quipped, "Don't you have a clean-air ordinance in this state?" Everyone was so shocked that there was dead silence drop.

It was then that Eddie noticed the "Jesus Is the Answer" sticker on Steve's notebook. "Are you a Christian?" asked Eddie as the bell was ringing.

"Sure am," replied Steve. "Are you?"

"Yes," Eddie smiled, "and I've been praying for a Christian friend at school."

✔ Putting the Truth Into Practice

Do you, like Eddie, need to make an exit from the group you're hanging around with at school? Are you being influenced by a non-Christian friend? Are you unwilling to identify with the Christians because everyone will think you're weird?

Surrender your friendships to God and make the necessary changes immediately. Ask God to choose your friends for you. He will.

CHAPTER 20

When Truth Lost the Debate

Jeff stared at the homework assignment on the blackboard. It was a "take-home exam" on the American Revolution—which would require about five hours to complete, and it was due the next day!

"Class," began Mr. Johnson, the history teacher, "when the answer sheet is missing and fifteen students get 100 on one of my tests, something's wrong. I don't like punishing the whole class, but unless someone tells me who stole the answer sheet, I have no other choice. I hate cheaters. And if you're all too chicken to rat on the guilty person, you all deserve to suffer."

Jeff was a Christian, and he hadn't cheated. But he knew that Tony had stolen the test. His locker was next to Jeff's and he'd overheard how Tony'd spotted the teacher's desk keys on the back table, pocketed them, and later sneaked across the street to the hardware store to have copies made.

Jeff had gone to school with Tony since the fourth grade. Tony was a slow learner and school was really hard for him. Jeff had heard that Tony's alcoholic father had threatened to kick him out of the house if he didn't bring home a B average. And everyone knew that Mr. Johnson's American history class was probably the toughest course in the whole school.

Afraid that his teacher might be able to see right through him, Jeff avoided Mr. Johnson's glance. If he told on Tony the guys would dump on him for the rest of the year. Yet, his conscience kept wrestling with him to tell the truth. Then his reasoning took over.

"Poor Tony. If my father were an alcoholic who was making it tough on me, what would I do? As a Christian I should have mercy—and I really do feel *sorry* for Tony. Besides, his dad would probably beat him up if he got suspended or expelled for stealing a teacher's keys."

So Jeff turned off the debate he was having with himself and started in on the gigantic assignment.

THIS WAY OUT

☞ Asking God to Meet Legitimate Needs

Sinning is *never* a legitimate need. Neither is helping someone else sin. God has created us to be dependent on Him, and He's arranged life so we must ask Him for help and wisdom—and miracles. If you or someone else has a big problem, the old formula "trust and obey" is the best. Disobedience to God's rules always brings ugly consequences. God cannot bless a person who steals money or cars or test answers. "Helping" a person get by with something wrong is not helping.

Stand up for truth and pray for God's solution to the problem.

Dear God, help me to do my part to see that justice is done—no matter what it costs me personally.

☞ Getting the Facts Straight

Do not follow the crowd in doing wrong. When you give testimony in a lawsuit, do not pervert justice by siding with the crowd, and do not show favoritism to a poor man in his lawsuit. (Exodus 23:2, 3)

God specifically tells us that we are not to permit pity or peer pressure to keep us from doing what is right.

It is not good to be partial to the wicked or to deprive the innocent of justice. (Proverbs 18:5)

Aquitting the guilty and condemning the innocent—the Lord detests them both. (Proverbs 17:15)

But it will go well with those who convict the guilty, and rich blessing will come upon them. (Proverbs 24:25)

And you can't get off the hook just because no one asked you a direct question. You are to do your part to convict the guilty. The success of justice in any country depends on people who are brave enough to speak the truth regardless of the consequences.

The teen culture has set its own rules, and according to the code turning in a friend who's done something wrong is one of the seven deadly sins. God's laws are exactly the opposite. You are commanded to convict the guilty.

Rethinking the Situation

Wally, the school engineer, was a family friend. Jeff's mom had a birthday present for Wally's wife, which she asked him to deliver to his office. Just as he turned the corner by the furnace room, Jeff literally bumped into Tony, who looked startled and seemed to be in a big hurry.

Wally came from the other direction and walked into the office at that same moment. "My keys!" he exclaimed. "They're gone!"

Jeff remembered what Tony had said to his friends at his locker. "In Richmond some kids snuck into the school and turned on the fire hoses and did so much damage that all the students got a three-week vacation. Pretty cool, huh?"

Now Jeff wished he had told on Tony before, but this time he would do what was right.

When Jeff explained the situation to Wally, a call to the office brought quick results.

The principal questioned Tony first, and then found the keys in his locker. Further investigation uncovered the scheme that Tony had concocted to enter the building at night and turn on the fire hoses.

Although Jeff was glad he'd turned Tony in this time, he couldn't help but wonder if the whole incident could have been avoided if he'd turned Tony in the first time.

☛ Putting the Truth Into Practice

You have to make up your mind that you're going to speak up for the truth regardless of what it will cost you—and it might cost an awful lot. Using only your human reasoning is always dangerous. Once you know the truth, you must decide to obey it.

There's a secret in 1 Peter 3:13 that you can put into practice:

> Who is going to harm you if you are eager to do good?

If you use the Miss Mouse or Peter Pussyfoot approach, you'll be ridiculed. But if by the power of the Holy Spirit you stand tall and speak the truth with conviction, you'll be respected.

CHAPTER 21

Danger Signs and Danny's Downfall

Danny's heart ached with loneliness. After three weeks in Los Angeles, he didn't have one friend. In fact, nobody in the ninth grade had even noticed him. Every day he found his way from class to class, ate lunch alone, and walked home by himself. His mom was too busy complaining about the neighborhood to talk with him much, and his little brother spent all his time in front of the television. His father's job promotion, the cause of all the misery, kept his dad in the office ten hours a day—even on weekends.

On Friday afternoon, Manuel approached Danny's locker. "Hey, what's your name?"

Danny told him his name and volunteered, "We just moved here from Oregon."

"You look like a cool dude!" Manuel exclaimed. "The group of guys I hang around with has something great planned for tonight. Why don't you come with us."

Although something made Danny feel uneasy, his longing for acceptance outweighed his fears. "Sure," he replied.

At 5:30, Danny met nine guys at the bus stop to go across town. The bus let them off in front of a rundown-looking restaurant that had a "Senior Citizen's Special" sign in the window.

Manuel said, "Danny, all you gotta do is ask some old lady for change for a five. Tell her you need it so you can take the bus home."

The other guys had gone to hide behind some bushes, and Danny was getting scared. He wasn't sure what was happening, but he had to stay with the gang because he didn't even know how to get home by himself.

Politely Danny approached a lady with a cane and asked her for change.

Suddenly, Manuel snatched the lady's purse, swiped her wallet and ran, leaving the purse on the sidewalk.

Danny was just as surprised and confused as the lady. But he had enough presence of mind to pick up her purse. She obviously had no idea that he had any connection with the thief, and she thanked him over and over.

When she went inside the restaurant to call the police, Manuel motioned for Danny to come, and they all scurried to McDonald's where the old lady's money bought them an all-you-can-eat supper.

"Danny, you were just great! That lady thinks you're a hero. You're the best help we've ever had."

Danny had to admit he enjoyed the feeling of acceptance. It was better than being a lonely ninth-grader. Belonging to a group and being praised felt great.

☑ Asking God to Meet Legitimate Needs

Dear God, you know that I need good Christian friends. I'm willing to make the effort. Just show me what to do.

☑ Getting the Facts Straight

My son, if sinners entice you, do not give in to them. If they say, "Come along with us . . . let's waylay some harmless soul . . . we will get all sorts of valuable things . . . throw in your lot with us, and we will share a common purse"—my son, do not go along with them, do not set foot on their paths. (Proverbs 1:10-16)

The temptation to run with a gang is not a new one. And the things that make it appealing are excitement, a sense of power, and a tightly knit peer group that offers belonging and approval. Solomon warns his son that once such a group rejects society and becomes a law unto themselves, they'll stop at nothing to achieve their goals.

Do not set foot on the path of the wicked or walk in the way of evil men. Avoid it, do not travel on it; turn from it and go on your way. For they cannot sleep till they do evil; they are robbed of slumber till they make someone fall. They eat the bread of wickedness and drink the wine of violence. (Proverbs 4:14-17)

If you start down the path of wickedness, it becomes more and more sinful. One's conscience can easily become hardened. Don't hang around with kids who don't have Christian standards.

Do not be overcome by evil, but overcome evil with good. (Romans 12:21)

✔ Rethinking the Situation

Danny became a faithful member of the gang. At first he had pangs of guilt, but after a while it didn't bother him anymore. Soon, they graduated from purse-snatching. Stealing cars, repainting and selling them was much more profitable.

Eventually, they tried armed robbery. One evening they decided to hold up a pharmacy. What they didn't know was that the unassuming elderly druggist kept a revolver on the shelf under the cash register— and he was a good shot.

Before anyone knew what was happening, one guy took a bullet in the chest. A police cruiser was nearby, and the whole gang got caught.

Behind bars, Danny had plenty of time to reflect on the path of wickedness. What he'd chosen initially, as a ninth-grader who needed acceptance, had become a way of life. The broad way had become wider and wider. Somehow defiance of authority, danger and getting money without working for it had gotten into his blood.

✒ Putting the Truth Into Practice

There's something about going where the action is with a group of young people that causes you to lose both your head and conscience. You can probably think of several things you've done under the influence of a group that you never would have dreamed of if you'd been alone. If the atmosphere is not good, stay away. Don't hang around with kids who don't have Christian standards.

You need friends who will help you do what's right. Seeking out a positive peer group may take a lot of time and effort. Maybe you'll have to call every gospel-preaching church in a new city to ask if they know of any Christian kids who go to your school. Be faithful to your youth fellowship, and if your church has nothing for young people, volunteer to organize some events. If there's a Christian group in your school, join it. If not, find other Christians in your school and start one. (Below are addresses of organizations that might help you.)[1]

Save your money and do everything possible to attend Bible camps, youth conventions, retreats and other Christian activities.

---

[1]Student Venture, 17150 Via Del Campo Suite 200, San Diego, CA 92127 Tel.: (619) 487–2717. Youth for Christ, 360 Man Place, P.O. Box 419, Wheaton, IL 60189 Tel.: (312) 668–6600. Young Life, 720 W. Monument, P.O. Box 520, Colorado Springs, CO 80901 Tel.: (719) 473–4262. Youth Specialties, 1224 Greenfield Drive, El Cajon, CA 92021 Tel.: (619) 440–2333.

CHAPTER 22

The Syndrome of Self

Mason was the only child of parents whose professions absorbed almost all their time. His father was a top executive and his mother was a director of nursing at a large hospital. Because they felt a sense of guilt for not spending more time with their son, his parents mostly let Mason have his own way. An intellectual, Mason buried himself in books and played "brain games" against the computer. What he enjoyed most was chess. He was a member of the chess club at school and he had won several championships.

Although Mason was lonely, he wasn't very good at making friends. Phil, a guy from church, noticed how sad Mason seemed and invited him home for dinner. He really enjoyed sitting around the table with a big family. The food tasted so much better than what he heated up in the microwave at home.

After that, he kept finding excuses to show up at Phil's house just in time to eat. Finally Phil's father told him straight out, "Young man, I'm going to treat you like my own sons. I instruct them to be polite and considerate of others. That's part of being a Christian. One of the rules here is: You never go to someone else's house at mealtime unless you're invited."

Mason felt hurt. He started avoiding Phil.

From then on, he turned his attention to Craig, whose father was one of the richest men in the city. Because Craig wanted to learn how to play chess, he welcomed Mason's friendship. He drove Mason around in his new Triumph and took him to eat in expensive restaurants. But one day, after an argument, he told Mason where to get off.

"You're nothing but a leech. You don't care about me. You just like my money."

Mason flared, "I could have charged you $15 an hour for chess lessons. Maybe then you'd owe *me* money." And so another friendship was terminated.

When Ginger, a pretty redhead, decided to join chess club, Mason offered to teach her how to play. Although she was a hopeless case when it came to learning chess, she was fun to be with. Soon they were dating regularly.

Mason tended to be possessive and jealous. He didn't like it when Ginger talked with other guys. Dates always centered around *his* interests—basketball games, chess tournaments, and eating Italian food. Mason was quick to notice her mistakes and good at pointing out her faults. He tried hard to squeeze her into his mold. Compassionate, easygoing, and accepting, Ginger chose the path of least resistance. When she suggested going to a Chinese restaurant, he put up a dozen excuses and took her to Angelo's instead.

One evening, when Ginger complained about their relationship, Mason got on Ginger's case.

She burst into tears, and then exploded. "Mason, you're self-centered, critical and obnoxious! You *never* think of my interests, or my feelings. Take me home right now. I don't want to go out with you ever again."

When he tried to calm her, she only sobbed. "Take me home. Take me *home*."

When she jumped out of the car, she slammed the door and ran into the house. Mason didn't know what to do.

THIS WAY OUT

☑ Asking God to Meet Legitimate Needs

You need God's help to be a friend, to learn how to sense the needs of others, to think of your friend's happiness first, and to accept constructive criticism. If you're spoiled, a loner, or from a family with serious problems, you probably have some handicaps in the area of knowing how to be a friend. But by recognizing unhealthy behavior patterns, asking God for wisdom and power, and then applying appropriate scripture to your life, you can change.

Dear God, show me how to be a true friend. Pinpoint areas of selfishness in my life and help me change.

☑ Getting the Facts Straight

Seldom set foot in your neighbor's house—too much of you, and he will hate you. (Proverbs 25:17)

Don't be a pest or a leech.

If a man loudly blesses his neighbor early in the morning, it will be taken as a curse. (Proverbs 27:14)

Be careful to sense your friend's mood and his or her need at the moment. Don't stick to your own agenda—however well-meaning you may be—without finding out how your friend feels about it. Be appropriate.

Don't use friendship for your own ends. Real friendship is basically getting from God so you can give to others.

Better is open rebuke than hidden love. The kisses of an enemy may be profuse, but faithful are the wounds of a friend. (Proverbs 27:5, 6)

As iron sharpens iron, so one man sharpens another. (Proverbs 27:17)

All of us need close friends who will be completely honest with us. Pay attention when others point out your faults.

An unfriendly man pursues selfish ends; he defies all sound judgment. (Proverbs 18:1)

If you're basically self-centered, you're not a good friend—no matter how charming and witty you may appear. Wanting all the attention, calling all the shots, or bossing everyone else around will only destroy true friendship.

118

✍ Rethinking the Situation

Phil had finished basketball practice and was returning to his locker to pick up his math book. As he walked down the hall, he looked into the room where the chess club met. There was a familiar face.

Mason was sitting there alone, slumped over an unfinished game of chess, looking as if he had lost his last friend. In fact, he had.

Phil walked in and invited Mason to his house for dinner.

On the way home, Phil asked enough questions to find out what Mason's problem was. Finally, Phil cleared his throat. "You're not going to like what I have to say, but I care about you and must tell you the truth.

"You don't know how to be a friend. You treat people like pawns on a chessboard. You think of what you can get out of them, and never what you can give. If you can't be in charge, you go on to someone else whom you try to boss. Ask God to give you His wisdom and start studying the Bible verses on how to get along with other people. If you're willing to learn, I'll help you. And you could start by not dominating the conversation at the dinner table."

Mason knew that Phil was right and he was willing to take drastic steps to change. And that evening for the first time in his life, he really tried to listen to the others and become interested in what they were saying.

✍ Putting the Truth Into Practice

Be daring enough to ask your three best friends what you could do to become a better friend. Write down their suggestions and prayerfully seek God's guidance. Study the life of Jonathan, who was an exemplary friend. (See 1 Samuel 18:1–4; 19:1–7; 20:1–42; 23:15–18.)

CHAPTER 23

Friendship and Forgiveness

To Angela, this was the last straw. Tina had borrowed Angela's English book and lost it. She didn't seem the least bit concerned that Angela had to walk half a mile to Jennifer's house to do her assignments until the special order of books came in. And she didn't offer to pay $15.95 to replace it either.

Although they'd been friends since seventh grade and Tina was also a Christian, Angela didn't really want to forgive her. She knew that Tina's parents were unbelievers who were very careless about paying debts, returning things borrowed and attending to details. But she wasn't ready to excuse Tina on that account. Tina had gone on a ski weekend, so Angela had until Monday to make her decision. She thought she'd just stop speaking to Tina.

Because her mom kept the dial tuned to the local Christian radio station, Angela heard a sermon while she cleaned the living room on Saturday morning.

"Broken friendships among Christians are tragic," the man was saying. "And most of the problems come because we don't know how to iron out differences in a godly way. Ephesians 4:15 recommends that we speak the truth in love. Matthew 18:15 also instructs us: 'If your brother sins against you, go and show him his fault, just between the two of you.'

"This loving confrontation will help you to keep from harboring bitterness and from cutting people off. It will also aide the other Christian who needs to deal with certain sins—if you come with a loving, forgiving attitude. And no matter how many times your brother sins against you, you are to forgive."

Angela's conscience started bothering her.

At 9:30 on Sunday evening, the phone rang. It was Tina. "Angela,

I'm so glad you're home. My parents are out. We're stuck on the freeway in front of the Carriage Inn. I ran out of gas. Could you bring me a couple gallons?"

Inside, Angela was fuming. That was just like Tina—irresponsible and asking for help. Angela was studying for her first hour Spanish test and she didn't feel like bailing Tina out.

THROUGH CHRIST JESUS THE LAW OF THE SPIRIT OF LIFE SET ME FREE FROM THE LAW OF SIN AND DEATH

ROM 8:2

SELF

SELF

THIS WAY OUT ➡

☑ Asking God to Meet Legitimate Needs

Learning how to forgive is basic to Christian living. It will also help you avoid ulcers, indigestion and insomnia. If you decide not to pardon those who wrong you, you'll have very few friends. But when you're *willing* to forgive, God will supply the grace you need. And don't worry about your emotions. They'll catch up with your will sooner or later.

Dear God, I will to forgive _____ . I don't feel like it, but I won't let my emotions run my life. Show me how I can show kindness to _____ .

☑ Getting the Facts Straight

He who covers an offense promotes love, but whoever repeats the matter separates close friends. (Proverbs 17:9)

You cover over an offense with forgiveness and you don't keep bringing it up again and again. This verse does not recommend sweeping everything under the rug. You deal with the situation *once* truthfully and lovingly and then you forgive and forget.

Watch out for any excuses you may manufacture because you don't feel like forgiving. Unwillingness to forgive causes disastrous results.

> But if you do not forgive men their sins, your Father will not forgive your sins. (Matthew 6:15)

> A friend loves at all times. (Proverbs 17:17)

> It is more blessed to give than to receive. (Acts 20:35)

If your idea of friendship is 50–60, forget it. Going the extra mile, turning the other cheek, paying more than your share—that's what Jesus taught. It's just that if the motivation, the willingness and the power don't come from the Author of this type of lifestyle, it won't work.

✔ Rethinking the Situation

Angela remembered the words she'd heard on the radio: "Broken friendships among Christians are tragic." She asked Jesus to give her His love and forgiveness for Tina. On the phone with Tina, she answered, "I'll get my brother to drive me. We'll be right over."

The next day, Angela had a talk with Tina. Gently, she explained what was bothering her.

"I'm sorry," Tina said quickly. "I honestly never thought of paying for the book. Here's $20, and I'll lend you my book until the order comes in. I can go to the resource room after school, since I don't have to catch a bus."

Angela had to love Tina for her ready generosity. How thankful she was that she hadn't avoided the issue, or just given Tina the cold shoulder. She knew that "speaking the truth in love" wouldn't always be this easy, but she determined to do it anyway.

✔ Putting the Truth Into Practice

1. List the problems you have with your friends.
2. Genuinely forgive each person who has wronged you.
3. Pray every day for a week that God will give you wisdom in handling any friction.
4. Arrange a "loving confrontation" if that is necessary.

CHAPTER 24

Betrayed

Although they were very different, Dixie and Shannon were good friends. Dixie was quiet and cautious, while Shannon was vivacious and outgoing.

They balanced each other out and learned things from each other.

One Friday, Shannon invited Dixie to spend the night. Usually they found a hundred things to talk about, and their laughter and giggling brought Shannon's mother to the bedroom door with her prerecorded message: "Girls, quiet down. Other people are trying to get some sleep."

But tonight was different. Dixie was depressed and distracted. She couldn't put her heart into anything. Shannon was concerned. "Something's bothering you," she prodded. "Maybe if you told me what it is, I could help you, or at least we could pray about it together."

"It's real personal," Dixie hesitated. "I don't know if I can confide in anyone."

"I won't tell a soul," Shannon promised. "And sometimes it helps just to talk about it."

"Well," Dixie stammered, "my parents think that my brother Daryl, who's away at college, is gay." And with that she burst into tears. Between sobs she managed, "My dad is angry and my mother cries all the time. My little brother Rusty's scared—and I don't know what to do."

"God does," Shannon soothed. She offered to pray for Dixie.

A week later, Rachel came up to Dixie and put her arms around her. "I'm praying for you," she said. "I don't know what I'd do if I found out my brother was gay."

☞ Asking God to Meet Legitimate Needs

Dear God, let me sense the security you give and your constant care so that I won't crave the attention that divulging secrets and spreading gossip can give me. Help me to keep every promise. Keep me from betraying my friends by telling the things I've pledged to keep secret. Keep me from giving broad hints or indirectly supplying the grapevine with confidential information.

☞ Getting the Facts Straight

A gossip betrays a confidence; so avoid a man who talks too much. (Proverbs 20:19)

A gossip betrays a confidence, but a trustworthy man keeps a secret. (Proverbs 11:13)

But the fruit of the Spirit is love, joy, peace, patience, kindness, goodness, faithfulness, gentleness, and self-control. Against such things there is no law. (Galatians 5:22)

Part of wisdom in friendship is being very careful about entrusting your secret to another. Obviously, a person who loves to gossip cannot be your intimate friend, because part of close friendship is confiding in each other.

Even people with good intentions can fall down in this area though, and there are some things that you should share only with God. If your secret could cause pain and harm if it were broadcast, it's wise not to trust another person with it—unless you're absolutely sure that it will go no further.

To be a good, trustworthy friend you must be able to keep a secret. Part of the fruit of the Spirit is self-control. If you let the Holy Spirit monitor your mouth, you'll leave a lot of things unsaid.

✔ Rethinking the Situation

Dixie was stunned—and deeply hurt. She felt betrayed. For days she avoided Shannon. Finally, Shannon came over to her house to ask forgiveness.

"But, Shannon," Dixie protested, "there's no way you can undo the damage you've caused. You've ruined the reputation of my whole family. What if our suspicions aren't true? Because everyone here thinks Daryl's gay, his summer vacation will be terrible—regardless of the facts."

"Please forgive me," Shannon pleaded. "I'm really sorry."

"I'm a Christian and I have to *forgive* you," Dixie said simply. "But I'll never *trust* you again."

After a few weeks, Dixie realized that she hadn't meant it when she told Shannon she was forgiven. Dixie was becoming more and more bitter and she keep thinking that Shannon didn't deserve to be forgiven. But Dixie knew that she herself didn't merit God's forgiveness. If God had forgiven Shannon, who was she to declare her perpetually guilty?

Dixie knelt by her bed and prayed, "I *will* forgive Shannon. Jesus, please heal the hurt—and the fear I have of ever trusting anyone again."

✔ Putting the Truth into Practice

1. Ask God's forgiveness for any confidences you have betrayed. Apologize to the people you've hurt.

2. Ask the Holy Spirit for His control over your mouth. Determine never to divulge a secret again.

3. Resolve that you'll be very careful about sharing any information you want held in confidence.

CHAPTER 25

The Story That Grew

Ray was the best-looking guy in the youth group. Athletic, outgoing and considerate, he was the favorite of the girls. Marji let everyone know she had a crush on him.

Hannah, Marji's friend, had also liked Ray for *two years!*—but she was painfully shy. Nobody knew her secret, or the bitterness she felt because of not having been noticed by Ray or any other of the boys.

When Ray started dating Lori, Marji was heartbroken. She knew that God's will might be different from hers, yet she had a hard time seeing Ray and Lori together—and she and Lori didn't know what to say to each other anymore.

One Friday night Marji and Hannah went out for ice cream. It was a little past 10:00 as they drove by a big downtown hotel where they saw Ray and Lori walking into the lobby. "What on earth are Ray and Lori doing at a hotel?" Hannah wondered out loud.

"Maybe they're going out to eat," Marji answered as she turned the corner.

"I wonder," Hannah said with a hint of suspicion.

A couple weeks later, Marji got a call from a girl in her church class. "Did you know that Ray and Lori spent a night at the Ambassador Hotel?"

"Who told you that? And how do you know it's true?" Marji asked.

"I heard that Hannah's cousin works there as the desk clerk, and he checked them in."

"I can't believe it!" Marji shot back. "But then, Hannah and I *did* see them walking in."

Before Saturday's youth meeting, Ray's best friend called Marji aside. "Marji, I can't believe it but everyone says that you've been spying on Ray and Lori and that you're trying to break them up by saying they spent the night in a hotel."

"That's not true," Marji replied angrily.

But Lori and Ray believed that Marji had started the rumor, and they stopped talking to her.

Soon the youth group was divided into two camps—those who defended Ray and Lori, and those who believed they were sleeping together and didn't think Ray should be president of the youth group anymore.

THIS WAY OUT

✔ Asking God to Meet Legitimate Needs

Dear God, help me to always put circumstances in your hands and never resort to the power of gossip to take revenge or change things. Show me how to guard my tongue and my ears. Keep me from listening to rumors and spreading them. Help me to never say anything that might be misinterpreted. Show me how to investigate and find out the truth so I can stop false reports.

✔ Getting the Facts Straight

Without wood a fire goes out; without gossip a quarrel dies down. (Proverbs 26:20)

The words of a gossip are like choice morsels; they go down to a man's inmost parts. (Proverbs 18:8)

A perverse man stirs up dissension, and a gossip separates close friends. (Proverbs 16:28)

There are six things the Lord hates, seven that are detestable to him: . . . a false witness who pours out lies and a man who stirs up dissension among brothers. (Proverbs 6:16, 19)

Gossip is a top cause of destroyed friendships, and losing a Christian friend is a tragedy. One of the seven sins God especially hates is sowing discord among people who are part of God's family. A few do it on purpose, but most simply pass on information or opinions without carefully checking the facts.

The best definition of gossip I've ever heard is this: "Sharing privileged information with someone who is neither part of the problem nor part of the answer."[1]

Be very careful about what information you give others. Remember you can even share a prayer request for a person without passing on all the details. God already knows what the problem is.

Rethinking the Situation

The dissension in the youth group reached the ears of the pastor. He took quick action. First, he called Ray and Lori into his office to ask them what the truth really was. They explained that Lori's uncle had come into town for an important business convention. He had meetings until 10:00 P.M., but had wanted to meet Ray, so he'd invited them up to his room.

Next, the pastor interviewed Lori's parents and Ray's parents who verified the story. He also confirmed that none of the desk clerks on duty that night was a cousin of Hannah.

After a convicting message on the evils of gossip, he asked, "How many of you told someone that Ray and Lori spent the night at a hotel, without checking the facts?" Several girls and two guys raised their hands. He told them to ask forgiveness of God, and of Ray and Lori.

Then he requested everyone to take their seats and to maintain prayerful silence. "I want every head bowed and every eye closed. I want the person who jumped to conclusions and started this rumor to confess. We're not here to judge you or condemn you. Obviously, if others hadn't passed on the report, no damage would have been done. It's just that you need to clear things up with God so you can start over again. If this false report originated with you, please stand up."

[1]Used by permission of Institute in Basic Life Principles.

At first, no one moved. Finally, Hannah began to sob as she rose to her feet. She asked everyone, especially Ray and Lori, to forgive her.

In time, God restored the love that gossip had robbed from the youth group.

✔ Putting the Truth Into Practice

Become a GBI (Gossip Bureau of Investigation) agent. A pastor I know of has a policy for letters he receives with negative information. He calls the person and asks permission to use his or her name publicly as the source of the report. Almost everyone he contacts admits that the truthfulness of the disclosure is in doubt.

You might ask your friend, "Will you give me permission to tell so-and-so that you told me this about him?" If they hesitate, you might ask, "How do you know it's true?" If there are enough GBI agents, the grapevine won't function very well.

Self-Examination

Part II: Love and Friendship

REPORT CARD

UNSELFISHNESS	C
CONSIDERATION	B
GENEROSITY	D
ACCEPTING CRITICISM	F
LISTENING	D

1. What kind of person should you date?

_____ a. One who makes decisions only after considering all the consequences.

_____ b. One who gives constant compliments.

_____ c. One who carefully follows all of God's commandments.

_____ d. One who puts God first, even ahead of you.

2. What is *the* reason for avoiding sexual immorality?

_____

3. God prohibits sex outside of marriage because

_____ a. He's a meany who doesn't want you to have any fun.

_____ b. He wants you to enjoy maximum sexual pleasure—at the right time with the right person.

_____ c. immorality brings serious health risks.

_____ d. memories of sexual sin can make your marriage more difficult.

4. "Bad c _____ corrupts good c _____" (1 Corinthians 15:33).

5. "But it will go well with those who c _____ the guilty and rich b _____ will come upon them" (Proverbs 24:25).

6. Why should all your close friends be Christians?

_____ a. Your friends automatically influence your thinking.

_____ b. Non-Christians don't have the same standards as Christians.

_____ c. It is very difficult to stand alone against a peer group.

_____ d. Then you can depend on your friends to lead you on the right path.

7. Rate yourself 1–10 on these qualities of a good friend:

_____ I am unselfish and generous.

_____ I'm not a pest or a leech.

_____ I'm careful to sense the mood of my friends instead of following my own agenda.

_____ I don't take advantage of my friends.

_____ I listen open-mindedly to my friend's constructive criticism.

_____ I'm careful not to dominate conversation or in another way make myself the center of attention.

_____ I ask my friend what he or she thinks or wishes to do instead of trying to call all the shots.

8. "But if you do not f _____ men their sins, your F _____ will n _____ forgive your sins" (Matthew 8:15).

9. A good friend must be able to keep a s _____ .
10. I'm sometimes a method of getting even. I'm very popular with insecure people who use me to get attention. I stir up dissention. I separate close friends. Who am I? _____

---

1. a, c, d; **2.** Because it's God's rule for your happiness written in the Bible; **3.** b, c, d; **4.** Company, character; **5.** Convict, blessings; **6.** a, b, c; **7.** Personal; **8.** Forgive, Father, not; **9.** Secret; **10.** Gossip.

Part Three

You and Your Work

CHAPTER 26

The Unending Nightmare

A little man knocked at the door, and when Ron opened it he was handed a sealed envelope.

With curiosity, Ron read: "If you don't clean your room, return your overdue library books, finish your biology report, complete your back math assignments *and* take your grandmother to visit her friend as you promised two months ago, a hydrogen bomb will destroy your town. The deadline is Friday at 5:00 P.M."

Shocked and shaken, Ron wanted to ask the little man some questions, but he had disappeared.

Ron attempted to straighten up his bedroom, but some unseen force kept him glued to the TV set.

The next morning he just couldn't get out of bed and slept until 12:00 noon. When he picked up his pen to try to write his biology paper, it was so heavy he could hardly lift it. Frantically, he looked for the list of math assignments he hadn't turned in but he couldn't find it anywhere.

When his grandmother didn't answer the phone, he remembered that she was in New York for the week.

Time was passing, passing, passing . . . and still he sat in front of the TV set, unable to move, incapable of preventing approaching doom . . .

Ron woke up from his nightmare in a cold sweat. He thought, "I'm sure glad it was only a dream."

But he couldn't help seeing his messy room, the pile of books he needed to return to the library, the introduction to the fifteen-page biology report that was due in a week and the "fail notice" from his math teacher with a big check marked "assignments not handed in."

Instead of facing all this, however, he decided to turn over and go back to sleep. Whoever heard of getting up at 7:00 A.M. on a Saturday? But he started to dream once more. The little man was knocking on his door, and he just wouldn't go away . . .

✔ Asking God to Meet Legitimate Needs

Dear God, show me how to be a good worker and how to enjoy completing essential tasks. Help me to finish what I start and teach me not to try to get out of hard work.

✔ Getting the Facts Straight

Laziness is sin!

"Six days you shall labor and do all your work" is a command, not a suggestion. Disobeying it brings disastrous consequences to your health and happiness.

S. I. McMillen, a physician, writes: "We do not understand the chemistry involved, but it is a well-recognized fact that physical work is both a preventative and curative factor in a member of mental disturbances."[1]

> One who is slack in his work is brother to one who destroys. (Proverbs 18:9)

---

[1]S.I. McMillen, *None of These Diseases* (Old Tappen, N.J.: Revell, 1963), 121.

In the name of the Lord Jesus Christ, we command you, brothers, to keep away from every brother who is idle and does not live according to the teaching you received from us. For you yourselves know how you ought to follow our example. We were not idle when we were with you, nor did we eat anyone's food without paying for it. On the contrary, we worked night and day, laboring and toiling so that we would not be a burden to any of you. We did this, not because we do not have the right to such help, but in order to make ourselves a model for you to follow. For even when we were with you, we gave you this rule: "If a man will not work, he shall not eat." (2 Thessalonians 3:6-10)

If you don't learn how to work hard and put your best effort into everything you do, you not only disobey God, but you endanger your emotional stability, financial status and relationships with others.

✍ Rethinking the Situation

Ron thought of himself as naturally "laid back."

But one Saturday his mother marched into his room, turned off his TV show and cleared her throat. "I ran into Joe Wilson at the grocery store," she began. "I asked how you were doing in Sunday school class and he told me you hadn't filled out your lesson manual for *six months*." Raising the volume, she continued, "You're not going to bed, or watching TV, or leaving your room until you've finished this week's lesson. Just give me a yell when you're done, and I'll come up to check it. Then you can get your freedom back."

Ron thought of a lot of excuses and wanted to beg to finish his program as he usually did, but he could tell by his mother's tone of voice and the look in her eyes that tonight he didn't dare cross her.

So he rummaged through his desk until he found the manual. Then he rescued his Bible from under the bed and started in. The lesson was entitled "Call It Sin!"

The introduction read, "You may not be a drug addict or a thief. You may not smoke cigarettes or drink socially, but if you're letting things slide, shirking responsibility and trying to get out of work, you're living in sin! The Bible teaches that laziness is sin. Stop making excuses and face it."

That hit Ron right between the eyes. Reading the required Bible verses and filling in the questions brought even more conviction.

Finally, he bowed his head and prayed, "Lord, forgive me for the sin of laziness. Forgive me for making excuses to postpone getting at assignments and helping my mother around the house. Forgive me for doing what I *want* to do rather than what I *should* do. Forgive me for trying to get other people to do my work for me."

✔ Putting the Truth Into Practice

Come to grips with the fact that laziness is sin. Confess it to God and your mother and anyone else who has suffered because you don't like to work.

Decide to go after laziness with a sledge hammer. Attack disagreeable tasks. Volunteer for tough jobs. Determine to use your time wisely and set priorities. Take good care of your belongings and make good use of your money. Finish what you start. Today do *one* thing that you've been putting off. Tomorrow work on another.

Root out the weeds of laziness now before they overrun the flowers in your personality.

CHAPTER 27

Lion-Hunting Lessons

Spring came, and Ron's parents decided that he was going to be responsible for the yard work. They determined that neither of them would lift a finger—no matter how terrible it looked. The character development of their son was more important than what the neighbors thought.

"Ron," his mother commented one day, "you've got to spray those dandelions. They look dreadful."

"No they don't," Ron responded automatically. "I like yellow flowers. If they weren't considered weeds, people would plant them for their beauty."

Soon the grass was tall. When Ron's father complained that the yard looked like a jungle and suggested renting some cows to eat the grass, Ron replied that the lawn mower needed gasoline and that it was too dangerous to bring it home in the car. He didn't want to cause an explosion.

When Aunt Lillian arrived for a visit, she was horrified. "Ruth," she exclaimed, "how can you stand to have your neighbors see your yard? It's shameful!"

"We decided that Ron needed to see the results of his procrastination," his mother answered. "But so far, the experiment has been a complete failure."

But Aunt Lillian was a person who spoke her mind. When Ron got home from school, she met him at the door. "It's good to see you. I brought your birthday present—but I prefer to deal with some unpleasantness first. I never thought a relative of mine could be so lazy, so thoughtless and so selfish! Why on earth don't you keep up this lawn?"

"It's because I have a lot of homework and there's no gas for the lawn mower," Ron replied angrily.

"Hold on, young man," Aunt Lillian ordered. "Jump in my car this minute. We're buying gas for that lawn mower—and you're paying for it!"

Ron was so caught off guard that he obeyed.

After they returned, Aunt Lillian demanded to see his last report card and samples of his homework. After viewing all *C*'s and *D*'s (except for a *B* in gym), she boiled over. "Ron, you're just plain lazy. Your excuses are ridiculous! You're a disgrace to your family! You're breaking God's commandments, and the pretexts you give are outright lies. If you don't change, your life is doomed!"

THIS WAY OUT

✔ Asking God to Meet Legitimate Needs

Dear God, you know how easy it is to make excuses for my laziness and how often I resort to lying in order to make things sound better. Forgive me. Help me to honestly admit it when I slip up or shirk my duty. Show me how to do my work so well that no explanations will be necessary.

✔ Getting the Facts Straight

The sluggard [lazy person] says, "There's a lion outside!" or, "I will be murdered in the streets!" (Proverbs 22:13)

The sluggard says, "There is a lion in the road, a fierce lion in the streets!" As a door turns on its hinges, so a sluggard turns on his bed. The sluggard buries his hand in the dish; he is too lazy to bring it back to his mouth. The sluggard is wiser in his own eyes than seven men who answer discreetly. (Proverbs 26:13-16)

"There is little that can be done for the lazy. . . . He sticks to his bed like a door to its hinges. When you try to get him to do something, he simply vacillates. Like a door on its hinges he swings back and forth, never going anywhere. We can never make any progress with him. And we cannot tell him anything—he is wise in his own conceit. It is exasperating to work with a lazy person. Laziness creates some of the most preposterous excuses we can imagine. . . . The sad thing is that the lazy person believes his own excuses."[1]

It's as if the writer of Proverbs wants you to remember how the lion-in-the-streets type of excuse looks to others. Next time you're tempted to invent some insurmountable difficulty or danger to avoid a job you dislike, picture the lion in the street and turn off the chatter. If you and your bed have been seeing too much of each other lately, have the guts to get up at 6:00 A.M. some Saturday just to prove you can break a bad habit.

Realize that pride is a horrible looking cloak for laziness. So cut the excuses you've used to keep from exerting yourself. Dissertations on the dangers of workaholism aren't appreciated when they come from the lips of the lazy.

Rethinking the Situation

Ron could see how he protected himself from unpleasant tasks with a barricade of excuses. And his alibis weren't even true. He didn't really like dandelions. He wasn't afraid the gasoline he bought for the lawn mower would explode. He was just in the habit of saying whatever occurred to him to put off unwelcome physical activity.

Aunt Lillian was still standing there waiting for his answer. "You're right," he stammered. "I'm pretty lazy. And I make up excuses by the truckload. And I know that laziness and lying are sin."

With that he got out the lawn mower and started working. He didn't even stop for supper. When darkness fell, the front yard was mowed and raked and clipped. The backyard wasn't quite finished, but he'd complete it the first thing tomorrow after school.

---

[1]James T. Drapper, Jr., *Proverbs: Practical Directions for Living* (Wheaton Ill.: Tyndale House Publishers, Inc., 1971), 60.

Eating his micro-waved supper, Ron felt a sense of satisfaction he hadn't experienced for a long time. He vowed to wage war on excuses, and do his work.

✔ Putting the Truth Into Practice

The apostle Paul wrote this, "No, I beat my body and make it my slave so that after I have preached to others, I myself will not be disqualified for the prize" (1 Corinthians 9:27). Your body is great if it is under the lordship of the Holy Spirit. But if the body gets to rule, watch out!

If you've ever decided to run a certain number of laps, you've probably experienced how your mind wants to help your tired body by skipping a lap. Those who have tried to diet have faced a hundred mental excuses to grab just one more brownie. And there is no scarcity of pretexts for getting out of work.

Conquer the "lion-in-the-streets" mentality!

1. Write down the excuses you most often use to avoid disagreeable tasks. (You may have to record them as you catch yourself fabricating another alibi. Some people are almost programmed to defend their laziness.)

2. Decide to eliminate all of them. (Maybe you need a "lion-in-the-streets" chart for each month. Every time you catch yourself with another excuse, put a lion in the street. In this case the goal of the lion-hunting expedition is extinction of the species!)

CHAPTER 28

Don't Blame the Devil for Something He Didn't Get to Do!

Al liked Sunday morning's sermon. The pastor spoke on "God's Advice on How to Get Rich." Although he daydreamed through the first part, he caught: "God promised to bless the person who tithes and is generous to others—if the rest of his life is consistent with his wisdom and His commandments. 'He who sows generously will also reap generously.' You can't outgive God. Those who make substantial investments in His kingdom prosper."

Al started his first job on Tuesday, and he decided to tithe regularly. He'd even give God some extra from his first paycheck. And he'd donate to the "Serving Seniors" organization his mom belonged to. He hoped that would bring instant prosperity.

Tuesday, Al learned how to fry hamburgers, how to clean the grill and how to mop the floor. He had to scrub the grill twice and mop the floor three times before the manager was satisfied. He left after 11:30, but was told that he'd only be paid for working till 10:00. If he was slow and inefficient, that was his problem.

Jack and Al worked together on hamburgers and French fries. Jack was a go-getter and he usually did most of the work while Al did most of the complaining. Being unaccustomed to discipline, Al thought he was doing too much.

One night, Jack went home sick and Al was stuck with everything. Halfheartedly, he began scrubbing the grill and he dreaded tackling the floor—at this rate he wouldn't get home until almost midnight. When the manager asked if he'd cleaned the floor yet, Al noticed that it looked pretty good. "Sure did," he replied, hoping his lie would go undetected.

Receiving his first paycheck, he triumphantly gave his tithe and an additional offering. He also made a contribution to help the senior

143

citizens. And he was excited about the wealth that would soon pour in.

Thankfully, Jack didn't get sick again, and they always worked the same shift. Doing as little as possible, Al mostly watched Jack work. Jack always mopped the floor, and he helped Al finish cleaning up the grill.

After a month, Jack was promoted to cashier, and Al was asked to train a new guy on the grill. For the first hour, he almost kept up with the orders—but finally everybody was yelling at him. In desperation, he served up half-done French fries and raw-in-the-center hamburgers. Complaints from the customers brought the manager to the scene. When he bawled Al out, Al shifted the responsibility to the new guy. And when closing time came, Al ordered the new guy to mop the floor and after that to clean the grill. Then Al sneaked out.

The next day, Al received a call from the manager. "You're fired. Don't bother coming back."

Al was furious! How dare the devil try to rob him of the blessing! He had tithed and was generous to others. He thought, "Maybe the Bible's got errors in it, after all."

THIS WAY OUT

✍ Asking God to Meet Legitimate Needs

Dear God, help me to face up to the consequences of my laziness head-on. I confess that I deserved _____ (low grade,

*getting scolded by my mother, getting chewed out by my boss, etc.)
because of my neglect and lack of diligence. Forgive me for saying
_____, which wasn't quite the truth, to cover up my
laziness.*

✔ Getting the Facts Straight

Lazy hands make a man poor, but diligent hands bring wealth.
(Proverbs 10:4)

Laziness brings on deep sleep, and the shiftless man goes hungry.
(Proverbs 19:15)

Whenever you want God's mind on a certain issue, it's necessary
to diligently study *all* scriptures that deal with the topic. Second Timothy 2:15 puts it this way:

Do your best to present yourself to God as one approved, a work-
man who does not need to be ashamed and who correctly handles
the word of truth.

It's a lot easier to grab a verse or two and base an entire doctrine
on a few words than it is to thoroughly search the Scriptures. And it's
a lot more dangerous.

According to the Bible, the prerequisites for God's prosperity
(which is not just material well-being but contentment and peace of
mind) include these: righteousness, application of God's wisdom, hard
work, responsibility, tithing, and generosity. And that doesn't mean
you may not be tested, like Job, or voluntarily give up great wealth
to serve God's people as did Moses.

Scripture clearly teaches that laziness will make you poor—
whether or not you tithe. God wants you to tithe but it won't cover
up for the basic dishonesty included in laziness. God can't put His
blessing on anything that lacks integrity.

Charles Spurgeon, a well-respected preacher of the past, has this
to say about the lazy person:

"A sluggard is not a righteousness man, and he cannot be; he
misses the main point of righteousness. It is very seldom that a sluggard is honest: he owes at least more labor to the world than he
pays. . . . He cannot be a righteous man, for slothfulness leads to
neglect of duty in many ways, and very soon it leads to lying about
those neglects of duty."[1]

---

[1]Charles Spurgeon, *The Bethany Parallel Commentary of the Old Testament* (Minneapolis:
Bethany House Publishers, 1985), 1238.

The poverty caused by laziness can be spiritual. Obeying God's Word demands effort. "Working out your salvation with fear and trembling" is not always convenient. It's all too easy for the lazy person to invent a theological excuse to justify his or her actions. After all, it's a lot easier than changing!

Laziness can also rob you of a rich social life. Negligent people find it hard to make lasting friendships. The work required to maintain good relationships is often more than they can handle.

✔ Rethinking the Situation

When 3:30 rolled around, Al's mother asked him why he wasn't going to work. Al responded with, "Satan just used my boss to attack me, now that I'm tithing and giving generously to the Lord's work. I lost this job—but I'm sure that God will provide me with something better."

Al went back to his room to watch TV, but his mother called his boss and asked why he was fired. When she hung up, she called Al into the living room.

"Al," she said sadly, "it's very dangerous to hold the devil responsible for your laziness and lying. Your boss told me that Jack always did your work for you and that you lied to him, telling him you'd mopped the floor when you hadn't. He said you were inefficient and that you blamed your mistakes on the new boy—and then left without even helping him clean up the mess. He couldn't keep you on any longer.

"You didn't listen to Pastor Jensen's sermon very well," she continued. "He listed several things that would make us poor. And the first one on the list was slothfulness. Then he gave the qualities of the person God promised to bless, and the first one he mentioned was diligence. You must obey God in every area or you'll be the loser."

At this point, conviction set in. Al was realizing more and more the deep roots that laziness had in his life. It had been easy for him to want a prosperity guarantee that bypassed hard work. He repented, and even called up his former boss to apologize for his lies. He said he knew he deserved to lose his job and thanked him for his patience.

Al made a very important decision. He realized that he had to learn how to work, and he volunteered to do the floor of his father's hardware store.

✍ Putting the Truth Into Practice

Are you poorer because of your laziness? Are you missing out on top grades, a good relationship with your parents or enjoying your job just because of your allergy to work? Worst of all, you may be poor spiritually, preferring a life of ease to diligent Bible study and prayer. Like Al, the slothful person is quick to blame God or "give up faith" because of jumping to unbalanced conclusions.

List the ways that laziness is making you poorer and more miserable. (Like, bad report cards; parents always on your back; frustrated friends because of procrastination in fulfilling promises; inability to give scriptural answers to your friends because of lack of Bible study.) Beside each, write down what you're willing to do to better the situation.

CHAPTER 29

The Gullible Gardener

Al had kept his job as a janitor in a rest home for six months. At last he'd learned how to mop floors and wash windows. But the routine of it all and the hard work required was getting him down, despite his recent commitment to work hard.

The lady who owned the place was very fussy and never failed to point out if he slipped up. How he longed to be able to call his own shots! He wanted a flexible schedule so he could spend time at the lake this coming summer.

Then he read a newspaper story that explained how two junior-high students in Florida had planted watermelons, and earned $2,000 in one summer selling them along the roadside. Al immediately decided that this was for him. His grandmother lived on a small farm, and now that his grandfather had died she'd welcome his using the garden.

He went out to buy watermelon seeds. After hearing a sales talk by the owner of the garden store, he also bought a deluxe tiller, because the man explained that it took the spading, hoeing, backache and hard work out of gardening. And that's what Al wanted.

Al's grandmother wasn't home, so he had the store delivery man leave the tiller in the field. He spent twenty minutes breaking up the ground, but then hurried home so he wouldn't miss his favorite TV program. He had plenty of time to plant those seeds—then all he'd have to do was sit back and wait.

When his grandmother called the house to ask what was going on, Al explained the whole scheme.

"But my dear boy," his grandmother worried, "Wisconsin doesn't have a long enough growing season to produce watermelons for two months. I'm concerned about the tiller out there in the garden. Someone might steal it, or it might get rained on. With my arthritis, I can't

148

move it. You should have asked me before going ahead with everything."

"Don't fret, Grandma," Al reassured. "Everything will turn out just fine. I'll be there after school tomorrow to work in the melon patch."

But the next day, Al's friends invited him out for ice cream and Al went along. There wasn't much daylight time left when he got home. And the following day he felt too tired to work. Then it rained for two days. Although his grandmother told him he had to protect the tiller, he didn't feel like going out in such nasty weather.

Three weeks later Al did do some work in his garden, but it was exhausting so he quit before he got very far. By the end of May, he had planted a few seeds. During the last two weeks of school he was too busy to even remember his melon seeds, and after that he gave himself a week to recuperate. Finally, he started in again. The tiller was beginning to rust from being outside all the time. Some of the seeds had come up—and so had a lot of weeds!

Although Al did end up planting all the seeds, he never quite got up the energy to attack the weeds. When his grandmother told him that his watermelon plants had "the blight" and needed to be sprayed, Al went with Barry to his cabin for a week. When he returned, someone had stolen his tiller, and most of his plants were dead or dying.

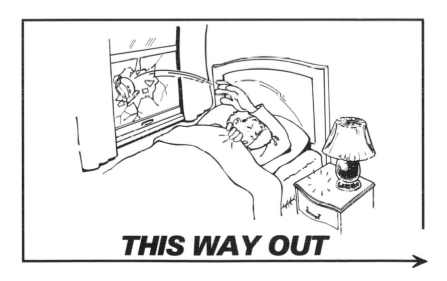

THIS WAY OUT ➡

▶ Asking God to Meet Legitimate Needs

How do each of these qualities relate to laziness?
1. Rash decisions.
2. Failure to plan ahead.
3. Desiring to be one's own boss.
4. Over-spending on labor-saving devices.
5. Procrastination.
6. A poor sense of timing.
7. Failure to properly care for possessions.
8. Dislike of schedules.
Why do you need to overcome each of them?

Dear God, help me to plan each decision carefully. Keep me from putting things off and arranging my private world around my convenience and my comfort. Show me how to live a disciplined life, because without it, I will never be able to be my best for you.

▶ Getting the Facts Straight

A sluggard does not plow in season; so at harvest time he looks and finds nothing. (Proverbs 20:4)

The plans of the diligent lead to profit as surely as haste leads to poverty. (Proverbs 21:5)

He who gathers crops in summer is a wise son, but he who sleeps during harvest is a disgraceful son. (Proverbs 10:5)

The lazy man does not roast his game, but the diligent man prizes his possessions. (Proverbs 12:27)

I went past the field of the sluggard, past the vineyard of the man who lacks judgment; thorns had come up everywhere, the ground was covered with weeds, and the stone wall was in ruins. I applied my heart to what I observed and learned a lesson from what I saw: A little sleep, a little slumber, a little folding of the hands to rest— and poverty will come on you like a bandit and scarcity like an armed man. (Proverbs 24:30–34)

Because his or her world revolves around making the present moment pleasant and easy, the lazy person exercises poor judgment. It takes work to make advance plans, so spontaneity is the order of the day. It's simpler to let things slide.

"The lazy person is too self-centered to be aware of time. He often does one thing when it is time to do something else. He latches the gate after the calf has already gone.

"Do you remember the story of the grasshopper and the ant? While the ant was working one summer, the grasshopper was out jumping around and having a good time. 'There is plenty of time,' the grasshopper told himself. When the cold weather came, the ant had prepared for winter, but the grasshopper had not. The ant went down into its warm cozy anthill. The grasshopper was left outside to freeze and die in the winter cold. The lazy man, like the grasshopper, flits here and there, never settling down to do the job that ought to be done."[1]

Rethinking the Situation

Al's grandmother invited him in to have a piece of German chocolate cake. As she poured him a big glass of milk, she began the conversation. "Al, you're a good boy and I'm glad to have a grandson like you. I want you to learn all you can from your gardening experience.

"You're old enough now to understand some things. You have wonderful parents—my daughter is a great mother—but they made one mistake. They spoiled you to the point that you know very little about work and responsibility. They thought they would never be able to have children and after you were born the doctor told them that another baby was out of the question. You were so precious to them that they gave you everything you wanted—without your having to work for it.

"Now that they've realized their error, it's hard for all of you to change. Don't blame them, though. You've had the good example of two hard-working people and the teaching of God's Word. Your bad habits are the result of your decisions.

"But as a result, you're facing life with a handicap. However, you *can* overcome it. I know you're a Christian and that you love the Lord. If I can just get you to see the dangers of laziness, you'll be willing to do anything to change. And God is ready to give you all the power you need. You spent a terrible lot of money on a machine that you thought could make up for your unwillingness to work hard. The slothful person often excuses himself because he doesn't have the right

[1]James T. Drapper, Jr. *Proverbs: Practical Directions for Living* (Wheaton, Ill.: Tyndale House Publishers, Inc., 1971), 63.

equipment. He tends to believe that a new gadget will solve every-thing, instead of admitting the real problem—laziness.

"Your schedule always centers around what *you want* to do, not what needs to be done. If you didn't feel like bringing the tiller into the shed, it stayed in the garden. If you wanted to do something different, the seeds weren't planted and the weeds grew taller. Even when something as urgent as spraying came up, you allowed yourself a week's vacation! If you continue to plan your life around your comfort and convenience, you'll flunk out of college, you'll never hold a good job, and you'll have problems in your marriage."

Seeing the picture his grandmother painted really shook Al up. He'd been blind to the incredible ramifications of his problem. He asked his grandmother to forgive him for not consulting her first, and he asked God to forgive him for wasting so much time and money.

🖝 Putting the Truth Into Practice

Although you may not have as much trouble as Al getting your act together, it's wise for you to have a strategy that will enable you to avoid jumping into projects which you may never be able to finish.

Project I Wish to Begin: _____

Advice on whether or not it is a good idea:

Parents	☐ Yes	☐ No
Christian leader	☐ Yes	☐ No
Someone who has done it	☐ Yes	☐ No

Tips on wise action:
Person 1
Person 2
Written material

Tips on actions to avoid:
Person 1
Person 2
Written material

Things you'll need:

What it will cost in terms of:
Money

Time

Deadline (If applicable):

CHAPTER 30

Even If It's a Matter of Life and Death

Al and two other high school guys were invited on a weekend camping trip by Dean, who was a young, single executive from their church. They weren't allowed to bring radios, flashlights or snacks. Instead, they'd hunt and fish and gather wild plants and berries to eat. In addition, they'd be doing some good Bible studies on the character of God.

They all rode in Dean's new car. Don and Brandon offered to help with the gas, but Al's watermelon fiasco had left him in debt, and his parents had decided that he was to earn all his own spending money. But he didn't feel bad about not chipping in for gas, because Dean made a lot of money and could well afford to help some poor high school guys.

Saturday morning, everyone except Al got up at 5:00 A.M. to go fishing. When Brandon tried to rouse him, he heard a grouchy, "This is vacation, man. And on vacation I sleep-in."

By 7:30 Al could smell the frying fish, so he dressed for breakfast. When they passed the plate, he took the two biggest pieces and didn't skimp at all on the blueberries. Sleeping in the great outdoors really gave him an appetite!

Dean sent Don and Brandon to get some wild rice he'd spotted, then asked Al to gather firewood. The trees in their autumn colors were spectacular so Al went exploring instead. On the way back he picked up a few dry sticks.

"Al," Dean moaned, "it takes at least forty minutes to cook wild rice, and what you've brought me will keep the fire going for a full two minutes."

Don and Brandon had returned with the rice, so Dean sent them to look for firewood.

After lunch they hunted rabbits, and gathered some edible greens which they could cook. After supper, the guys gathered firewood for breakfast and were given free time.

Later, the three decided to explore the caves by the lake. "Be sure to be back by 8:00," Dean cautioned. "You could get into trouble after dark."

Because they were enjoying themselves so much, though, they hardly thought of the time. Suddenly, Don stumbled and fell about twelve feet straight down. Blood covered his head, and it was obvious that he was seriously injured. He kept groaning, "Get a doctor, get a doctor."

"Run for Dean," Brandon ordered. "I'll stay with Don."

Al ran faster than he ever had in his life. Dean got the first-aid kit out of his trunk, then handed Al the keys.

"Take my car. Find the first phone, call an ambulance and tell them to hurry."

Al got into Dean's car and started out. Stopping at the first gas station, he asked where the nearest hospital was and if he could use the phone. "I'm sorry. It's out of order," the attendant answered.

Next he approached a farmhouse, but the lady wouldn't let him in.

Finally, he got to a town. The only thing open was a bar. There, he called the hospital, but the receptionist told him their only ambulance had just left on an emergency call and she had no idea when it would return.

At this, Al gave up and drove back.

Finding his friends in the cave, he explained the situation.

Dean was struggling to control his anger. "Why didn't you call another hospital? Why didn't you get a doctor out of bed? You're too lazy to get up early in the morning, too lazy to gather firewood, and too lazy to save your friend's life. Don's already slipped into a coma!"

☑ Asking God to Meet Legitimate Needs

Dear God, help me to see how selfish laziness can make me. Show me how my laziness hurts others. Lord, by your grace, I'm willing to change.

☑ Getting the Facts Straight

As vinegar to the teeth and smoke to the eyes, so is a sluggard to those who send him. (Proverbs 10:26)

The sluggard's craving will be the death of him, because his hands refuse to work. All day long he craves for more, but the righteous give without sparing. (Proverbs 21:25, 26)

Never be lacking in zeal, but keep your spiritual fervor, serving the Lord. (Romans 12:11)

"The lazy person is . . . unbelievably selfish. . . . He has no one else's interest at heart. He is not concerned for his fellowman, for the kingdom of God, for the righteousness of society or anything else except his own comfort . . . even worse, the lazy person is the last one to see what kind of person he is. Everyone else knows, but not him. He is too self-centered to see.

"What is the experience of the lazy person? 'The lazy man longs for many things but his hands refuse to work. He is greedy to get, while the godly love to give' (Proverbs 21:25, 26). He always wants the possessions or prestige that somebody else has. He craves the place of honor, the place of attainment, the place of favor in the eyes of men. This desire is his downfall."[1]

Laziness does not go the extra mile, does not do good to all people and does not give itself fully to the work of the Lord. And if the habits of laziness are deeply enough ingrained, even a life and death situation won't change them.

[1]James T. Drapper, Jr., *Proverbs: Practical Direction for Living* (Wheaton, Ill.: Tyndale House Publishers, Inc., 1971), 61.

◤ Rethinking the Situation

Al, Brandon and Dean sat in the hospital emergency room awaiting the doctor's report on Don. Nobody spoke, and Dean and Brandon were silently praying.

But for Al, prayer was impossible. Waves of condemnation swept over him. He was a leech and a quitter. Letting someone else do the work and reaping all the benefits was so natural to him that he never even thought of it as bad. Getting by without paying his share had brought him no shame—until now. And he was so accustomed to impossibility thinking and deserting as soon as something appeared difficult that he hadn't even thought twice about it.

Tears filled his eyes as he prayed, asking God to forgive him. Then he told Dean and Brandon that he was sorry for not doing his share of the work and eating the largest portions. Fervently, Al prayed that Don would live so he could apologize to him, too.

Then Al started to think of a long list of unselfish things he could do for others.

◤ Putting the Truth Into Practice

1. Write down the selfish acts that your allergy to work has perpetrated. (Like, making your mom do the dishes when she's overtired; disappointing your little brother when you watch TV instead of playing basketball with him, etc.)

2. Ask God's forgiveness.

3. Figure out a way to pay these people back by working for them. (Like, offering to do the dishes every day for a month; playing with your little brother right now.)

CHAPTER 31

Reaching the Finish Line

When he was a senior, Trent was elected president of the church youth group. Because the church was small, attendance ranged between ten and fifteen. Cory, who was very personable but not very faithful, was chosen vice president. Jan was reelected secretary and Cindi became treasurer.

Since the district youth retreat in October was always a highlight and the group wanted to provide scholarships for new kids, they needed a fund-raising project. Someone suggested selling microwave popcorn in small plastic bags at the mall. Jan got permission and invited everyone to come to her house on Saturday morning at 8:00. Three people promised to bring their microwave ovens so they could finish their work quickly and go to the shopping center to sell popcorn.

When Trent arrived at 8:30 with his mother's microwave oven, nobody else had shown up. Jan was already busy and had an impressive quantity of bagged popcorn on the counter. Ten minutes later, Cindi breezed in, explaining that she could stay for only a half hour.

After she left, Trent said, "Jan, this is ridiculous. Let's just throw this popcorn away and enjoy our Saturday. This is a *group* project, and it's not fair for two people to do all the work."

"Trent!" Jan exclaimed. "I'm surprised at you! Throwing away all this good popcorn would be wasting God's money. Besides, we're working for the Lord and *He* sees what we're doing."

"You can do what you want," Trent replied, "but I've got enough sense to give up a lost cause." With that, he left.

Jan went to the mall alone and stayed until she had sold all the popcorn.

Trent's next project was "Fasting for the Hungry." Everyone was to fast twice a month and contribute the money that breakfast and

158

lunch would have cost to a fund to help starving children. He set Friday as the first fast day.

By noon on Friday, though, even the school lunch looked appealing. His stomach was growling and he had a headache. So he not only ate everything on his tray but the three candy bars he had in his locker. And he never mentioned the plan again.

Instead, he focused on training groups of twos to go witnessing at "The Place," a popular teen hangout near their church. He invited a youth leader from a neighboring congregation to come and give them a month's course on evangelism. But when Trent saw how much homework there was with each session he began to lose interest. He stopped promoting the classes and let them die a natural death.

THIS WAY OUT →

Asking God to Meet Legitimate Needs

Dear God, show me how to invest my time wisely—and how to finish whatever I start.

Getting the Facts Straight

He who works the land will have abundant food, but the one who chases fantasies will have his fill of poverty. (Proverbs 28:19)

Be sure you know the condition of your flocks, give careful attention to your herds; for riches do not endure forever, and a crown is not secure for all generations. (Proverbs 27:23, 24)

The way of the sluggard is blocked with thorns, but the path of the upright is a highway. (Proverbs 15:19)

Someone has said, "Time is the stuff of which life is made." Letting hours and days slip by without accomplishing anything means wasting part of your life. Seeking God's wisdom for initiating the projects *He* wants you involved in, and then sticking with them until they are completed is essential if your life is to count for God.

First of all, you must honor God by doing your job well. In Bible times this work was agriculture. For you as a teenager your work, primarily, is school. Studying to please God and doing your best for Him is of utmost importance to your spiritual life. If you study hard only to prove yourself and get honors, you'll burn out and become frustrated. If you procrastinate and barely slip by, you'll not only miss out on a good education, but you'll form habits that will hurt you all your life. By offering your best schoolwork as a living sacrifice to God, you'll receive His blessing.

The lazy person imagines that there are hedges of thorns which block him from completing whatever work he begins, while the person who has learned righteous diligence trusts God for the energy, the intelligence, the tools, or the help needed to finish what's been started. The procrastinator finds the job harder than it would have been if he'd attended to it immediately, while the ambitious person seems to complete the task without effort. The procrastinator exerts more energy dreading the assignment than the disciplined student does in completing it.

Treat each undertaking in your life as a venture for God that merits your best work until it's finished.

☑ Rethinking the Situation

Because the pastor got on his case, Trent called a youth officers' meeting. "I've got a great idea," he began enthusiastically. "Our youth group could put on evangelistic puppet shows at the children's hospital." Jan's black eyes flashed fire.

"What's the matter?" Trent asked in surprise. "Don't you like my idea?"

Jan exploded. "You *never* complete anything you start. You're just too lazy. As soon as something becomes hard work, you quit. You're the most frustrating leader I've ever worked under. I'd like us to reach the finish line just once!

"Besides, the only reason there's any money in the treasury at all is because I went to the mall by myself and stayed until I sold all the popcorn instead of throwing it away like you suggested. You didn't even fast *one day,* and you didn't do your homework for the evangelism course. You're a bad example."

For a moment there was stunned silence. Then Jan recovered herself enough to apologize. "Trent, I'm sorry for getting angry—but I told you exactly how I feel."

"We all feel that way," Cindi put in. "No matter what you suggest, there won't be any enthusiasm. We're all bummed-out on unfinished projects."

Trent hung his head. "The Lord's been working in my life and convicting me of my laziness. I'm really sorry I failed you guys. I'm seeing more and more how it affects every area of my life. Jan, you're the most faithful worker in the group. Why don't you initiate a plan. Whatever you want to do, I'll get behind it. Maybe I can learn something about work—from an expert."

Putting the Truth Into Practice

1. Make a list of your unfinished projects.

2. Pray until you know which ones you never should have started and which ones you should still finish.

3. Ask God's forgiveness for wasting His time and His money on things that weren't really His will.

4. One by one, complete the other projects.

CHAPTER 32

A Job Well Done

At the next youth meeting, Trent announced that Jan had a project for the group. Jan explained that their denomination was sponsoring youth group quiz teams. The prize for winning locally was going to the summer youth camp free of charge. State winners were sent on a trip to Washington, D.C. Jan said that her cousin in Detroit had been on a winning team seven years before and that she would give them pointers. This year they were to study the book of James.

Response was enthusiastic, and Jan handed out workbooks on James that had to be completed in two weeks. "Do a chapter each day," Jan said, "and you'll finish three days early."

Trent did his chapter for two nights in a row. On Wednesday, he had to choose between two favorite TV programs and studying James. He started watching the tube and it took all the energy he could muster to turn it off and get to work. But he did it.

The next evening, he felt totally exhausted. He prayed for strength instead of telling himself it was impossible to work that night.

And on Friday, he turned down an invitation to go out for pizza— all so he could turn in his completed workbook on time.

Next, they were to memorize the entire book of James—all 108 verses! Half the group dropped out, and Trent was tempted to quit. But Jan said that by learning two verses a day they could complete it in less than two months.

They quizzed each other over the telephone and met twice a week to encourage one another. It was amazing how making a plan and sticking with it made a seemingly impossible job workable. Because he'd always been so lazy, Trent didn't even know that he was good at memorization. Actually, he learned the verses faster than the others. He began to enjoy it.

During Easter vacation, Jan's cousin came and drilled them for four hours every morning. Staying home to watch TV or sleeping in occurred to Trent, but by now he was able to resist these temptations. He was learning to carry his weight and take satisfaction in doing his best.

THIS WAY OUT

☛ Asking God to Meet Legitimate Needs

Dear God, help me to learn to give my best effort to everything I do. Teach me how to be a self-starter and to work without being told.

☛ Getting the Facts Straight

Go to the ant, you sluggard; consider its ways and be wise! It has no commander, no overseer or ruler, yet it stores its provisions in summer and gathers its food at harvest. (Proverbs 6:6–8)

Do you see a man skilled in his work? He will serve before kings; he will not serve before obscure men. (Proverbs 22:29)

All hard work brings a profit, but mere talk leads only to poverty. (Proverbs 14:23)

Whatever your hand finds to do, do it with all your might. (Ecclesiastes 9:10)

It's God's will that you be ambitious and hard working, that you learn to do things well—and that you bring glory to Him by the way you work.

⮕ Rethinking the Situation

When competitions began, they were all nervous and excited. Trent's team easily defeated the first two groups that went against them. Though the rivalry was intense, they became district champions.

During the week before going to state, Trent worked harder than he ever had in his life.

The state-wide competition was an unforgettable experience. Besides quizzing, they made new friends and listened to challenging messages each evening. By the end of the first day, Trent's team was still in the running. The second day, the contests were extremely fierce, but they won every round. This meant they'd quiz in front of the whole auditorium in the finals! Remaining cool, Trent was able to answer the only question the other side missed and that won them the state championship.

The rewards of hard work were indeed great—admiring friends, proud parents, plus the trip to Washington, D.C.! But most important, Trent had done his best to please the Lord. And it gave him a different self-image and a deeper determination to learn diligence in everything.

Trent thanked God for His patience and the hard lessons. They'd humbled him to the point where he was willing to learn how to work hard. A job well done was worth more than a thousand TV shows and a month of sleeping in.

⮕ Putting the Truth Into Practice

Do you, like Trent, need some organizational pointers to help you get your work done? After making your list of "Things to Do," ask some people who are good students and good workers for efficiency tips. Make some plans yourself. How many pages do you need to read each day to finish your library book in time to write a good report? What should you do each week in order to finish the science project on time? Make a schedule to guide your use of time.

Self-Examination

Part III: You and Your Work

DECODE the themes of each devotional in chapter three. (Each message is written in consonants only—like ancient Hebrew!) If you add the correct vowels, you'll get the point.

1. LZNSS S SN. Y MST CNFSS T GD ND CHNG. _____

_____

2. YR XCSS FR GTTNG T F WRK SND JST S CRNY S "THRS _ LN N TH STRT S __ CN'T." _____

_____

_____

3. LZNSS WLL CS PVRTY N YR FNNCS, YR SCL LF, ND VN

YR SPRTL LF. _____

4. RSH DCSNS, FLR T PLN HD, PRCRSTNTN, __ PR SNS F TMNG, ND DSLK F SCHDLS R CMPNNS F LZNSS. _____

5. LZNSS S VRY SLFSH. T THNKS FRST F PRSNL CMFRT ND S—NVR F TH WLFR F THRS. _____

6. LZNSS PRVNTS __ PRSN FRM FNSHNG WHT H R SH STRTS. _____

7. LRN T GV YR BST FFRT T VRYTHNG Y D—T GLRFY GD BY TH WY Y WRK. _____

8. "The f_____of the Lord is the b_____ of w_____ " (Proverbs 1:7).

9. Where will you find true wisdom? _____

10. Why does God prohibit sex outside of marriage? _____

---

1. Laziness is sin. You must confess it to God and change. 2. Your excuses for getting out of work sound just as corny as "There's a lion in the street so I can't." 3. Laziness will cause poverty in your finances, your social life, and even your spiritual life. 4. Rash decisions, failure to plan ahead, procrastination, a poor sense of timing, and dislike of schedules are companions of laziness. 5. Laziness is very selfish. It thinks first of personal comfort and ease—never of the welfare of others. 6. Laziness prevents a person from finishing what he or she starts. 7. Learn to give your best effort to everything you do—to glorify God by the way you work. 8. Fear, beginning, wisdom. 9. In God's Word. 10. Because He wants you to avoid problems and heartache and to enjoy maximum sexual pleasure at the right time with the right person.

CHAPTER 33

Robbing God's Bank to Buy a Blue Sweater

Stephanie sat with hundreds of teens at a city-wide rally. With a sense of satisfaction, she glanced down at her new skirt. Her shoes matched her outfit perfectly, and after saving her money for another week she'd be able to buy that blue sweater at Nordstroms to complete her newest outfit. She hoped she'd have some place special to go next Saturday night to be seen in it. Maybe that would lift the nagging depression she usually felt. Compliments always gave her a lift.

Her thoughts were interrupted by the laughter of the crowd, but she hadn't been listening, and missed the joke. Turning her attention to the speaker, she was surprised by his topic. He read from Malachi 3:8, 9. " 'Will a man rob God? Yet, you rob me. But you ask, "How do we rob you?" In tithes and offerings. You are under a curse—the whole nation of you—because you are robbing me.'

"Tithing," he then explained, "means giving God one-tenth of the money that passes through your hands. It's a special way of honoring God and putting Him first in every area of your life. The Old Testament talked a lot about tithing, and we know that Jesus believed in it.

"Some people call you guys the 'gimme generation,' " the man on the platform continued. "They say that selfishness is the trademark of today's teenager. Personally, I'm not so sure that the adults who accuse you are all that generous themselves. But there is a cure for self-centeredness. It's giving to God first and trusting in all His promises to supply your needs.

"Just listen to the rest of what God says in Malachi 3:10: 'Bring the whole tithe into the storehouse, that there may be food in my house. Test me in this,' says the Lord Almighty, 'and see if I will not throw open the floodgates of heaven and pour out so much blessing that you will not have room enough for it.'

"If you're faithful to God, He'll be faithful to you. He knows you need blue jeans, and hamburgers and tennis rackets. Trusting Him is a great adventure. Taking everything you can get and keeping it all for yourself gets boring, stale and unsatisfying after a while. Budgeting by faith means receiving from God and generously giving back to Him and to others. That will give you prosperity and the adventure of watching how God will return what you give to Him.

"In tonight's offering I'm asking you to give a tenth of the money you have with you. Start tithing now—not tomorrow or in a month or two. Begin enjoying God's bigger blessing on your life."

Although Stephanie felt convicted and guilty, she just couldn't part with any of her money. And that night she dreamed about robbing God's bank to buy a blue sweater.

THIS WAY OUT ➔

✔ Asking God to Meet Legitimate Needs

Dear God, give me that sense of significance I need so I won't depend on things to make me feel important. I know I can personalize your word, "But God demonstrates His love for ME in this; While _____ (your name) was still a sinner, Christ died for ME." I realize that I'm very important or you wouldn't have died for me. Thank you for your love and acceptance. I don't need to constantly buy new things so people notice me. Your approval is enough.

☞ Getting the Facts Straight

God knows all about your material needs. If you give to Him first, He'll take good care of you.

> But seek first his kingdom and his righteousness, and all these things will be given to you as well. (Matthew 6:33)

> Honor the Lord with your wealth, with the firstfruits of all your crops; [give God the first part of the harvest] then your barns will be filled to overflowing, and your vats [containers] will brim over with new wine. (Proverbs 3:9, 10)

A modern paraphrase might read, "Give God your tithe off the top and there will be plenty left over for sneakers, cassettes, and pizza."

☞ Rethinking the Situation

Stephanie sat in church on Sunday night wearing her beautiful blue sweater. Frankly, she was somewhat disappointed that more people hadn't noticed it. A rather poorly dressed lady was called to the platform by the pastor to give a testimony.

She said that she and her husband had four children and some unexpected expenses had strained their budget. But one week she babysat her friend's little boy. The money she earned was carefully set aside for a new dress—and she hadn't bought one in over a year. But then a representative of a ministry that distributed Bibles in Russia had spoken on the radio. He explained that his organization gave these Bibles as wrapped gifts and included the name of the sender.

The lady said, "At first I didn't want to give anything. But God impressed me to give all the money I'd earned. It was hard, but I obeyed. Just yesterday I received a letter from Russia. It said: "Thank you for sending me the Book that gave me the opportunity to know God. I've wanted to know Him for a long time, but I didn't have His Book.""

"I'm so excited," the woman continued. "A new dress could never give me the satisfaction I've gotten from investing in things that count for eternity."

Stephanie looked down at her blue sweater. She knew that the main reason she bought expensive clothes was that she craved compliments. Yet she really hadn't thought about receiving the approval of God. She tuned in on her pastor's sermon. "God loves us more than we could ever be loved by anyone. No matter who you are or

172

what you've done, God loves you." Stephanie started to feel the security of God's love. And when they took up the offering, she gave liberally. She really didn't need the new shoes she was planning to buy and the compliments they would bring. She loved God and knew that He loved her.

She just couldn't rob Him again.

☑ Putting the Truth Into Practice

List the things you'll have to change in your life to put Proverbs 3:9, 10 into practice.

_____

_____

_____

Suggestions:
   1. Decide to tithe without ever cheating.
   2. Give God extra love offerings.
   3. Expect Him to keep His part of the bargain.
   4. Pray for the things you need and want, then wait for answers.

CHAPTER 34

And the Trap
Started Closing In

Bobby came from a solid Christian family where he felt love and acceptance. Because there were six children and his dad didn't hold an executive position, Bobby couldn't help noticing that almost everyone else had the expensive clothes, the extra spending money and the vacations that his family just couldn't afford.

Bobby didn't like being the poorest kid on the block. He became secretly jealous and resentful.

In ninth grade, he met Jared, who was the only child of the owner of a chain of very popular restaurants. Because of their common interest in sports, they formed a fast friendship.

Jared invited Bobby to go skiing in the mountains. Bobby wanted to go, but he just didn't have the money to rent equipment and pay the tow ticket.

"No problem," Jared insisted. "I need new skis. I'll give you my old ones. And I can pay for both of us."

Bobby loved skiing! During Christmas vacation, Jared invited him to go with his parents for a week in Vail, Colorado—all expenses paid. Bobby could hardly believe it.

Because they knew that Jared and his parents weren't Christians, Bobby's folks gave permission for the trip reluctantly.

In Colorado, Bobby wasn't very comfortable with the atmosphere in the restaurants they ate in each night. But the steak and shrimp sure tasted good! Jared's parents drank and argued a lot, so Bobby fixed his thoughts on the food and the skiing.

Bobby started missing church to go on weekend ski trips. And when he was with Jared he skipped morning devotions, because somehow he felt embarrassed reading his Bible and praying when his friend was around. Not only was his spiritual life suffering, but he noticed

173

that Jared was becoming more and more possessive of his friendship. Jared did come to youth group meetings occasionally, but he resented it when Bobby gave his attention to some of the other guys. When Bobby declined an invitation to go bowling because it was his mother's birthday, Jared got angry.

"After all I've done for you, look how you treat me," Jared said sulkily.

THIS WAY OUT

Although Bobby was getting uncomfortable with the situation, he enjoyed all the expensive clothes Jared had given him and wasn't really content to go back to living on his small allowance. The invitation from Jared and his parents to go sailing on the Caribbean for a week was too good to turn down. His parents didn't want him to go because he'd miss Bible camp, but he finally convinced them by making them feel guilty because he had so much less than most of his friends.

And sailing was really exciting! The exotic tropical beauty of the islands captured Bobby. But in spite of all the excitement and fun, he couldn't help noticing that Jared was clinging to him in an unnatural way. And that night in their hotel room, Bobby realized that Jared was beginning to make advances on him. Bobby ran to the bar to find Jared's parents.

Both of them had been drinking. When Bobby accused Jared, his parents became furious. "After all we've done for you—you have the nerve to accuse our son?" Jared's father shouted. "You're going to be on the next plane out of here!"

The next morning, Bobby sat alone at the airport, confused, hurt, angry, embarrassed. What if Jared spread rumors about him? How he wished he could live the year over again.

▶ Asking God to Meet Legitimate Needs

Dear God, I know that "godliness with contentment is great gain" (1 Timothy 6:6). Help me to be satisfied with what I have so the devil can't use an unsurrendered desire to deceive me. Give me alertness to sense something is wrong so I can get back on your path the moment I start getting off-track. I determine to thank you for everything, even_____ and _____. You know that I need _____. I'm asking you to supply it.

Remember that sacrificing spiritual blessings, healthy friendships, or a well-balanced life for more money, more pleasure, or more possessions is always wrong. First Timothy 6:8–9 explain the problem:

But if we have food and clothing, we will be content with that. People who want to get rich fall into temptation and a trap and into many foolish and harmful desires that plunge men into ruin and destruction.

▶ Getting the Facts Straight

A prudent man sees danger and takes refuge, but the simple keep going and suffer for it. (Proverbs 22:3).

Folly delights a man who lacks judgment, but a man of understanding keeps a straight course. (Proverbs 15:21).

Your biggest danger is not that the devil will tempt you to commit murder or mainline heroine, it's the tendency to slip away from God little by little. The wayward wish which is not under the lordship of Christ blinds you to danger signs. By heeding God's warning signals you'll avoid a lot of hassle, hurt and heartbreak.

▶ Rethinking the Situation

When Bobby got back home he wanted to avoid everyone. His father finally sat him down and extracted the whole story.

"Son," he said quietly, "you're worried about the wrong thing. Proverbs 26:2 says that 'an undeserved curse does not come to rest.' Kids aren't going to believe that you're a homosexual—even if Jared spreads some rumor—which seems pretty unlikely.

"Your real problem is that pleasure and things are too important to you. God kept giving you warning signals all along the way, but your strong materialistic desires drowned them out. I may have given you too much freedom in making your own decisions. But if you learn a lesson from this experience, you'll spare yourself the other pitfalls caused by a craving for pleasure and things."

Bobby bowed his head and asked God to forgive him for not being content with the things he had. Then he turned to his father, "Dad, I'm sorry. I haven't appreciated your love and the fine Christian home I have. I'm sorry for expecting things that you can't afford to give me."

When school started, Jared was giving big presents and free trips to another guy. Bobby had decided to put God first, and his sophomore year was a lot better. He didn't even miss the things he once thought were so important.

▶ Putting the Truth Into Practice

What things are keeping you from going to church, studying the Bible and praying? Which activities are side-tracking you from serving God? These are potential problem areas. What wayward wishes could the devil use as the basis of deception in your life? A strong desire that is not under the lordship of Jesus Christ will drown out the warning signals God is giving you. Let Jesus give you a heart checkup and then surrender your will to His.

CHAPTER 35

Kicking the Habit

Larry and Nick were best friends. They hung around together at school, played tennis together. And when things got tough they prayed together.

One Monday after school, they stopped by Radio Shack. The new stereo receiver Larry had wanted for so long was on sale. By putting down $200 and paying the rest in monthly installments he could take it home that day.

"Nick, do you have any money on you?" Larry asked, turning to his friend.

"Yeah—most of my paycheck," Nick replied.

"Could you lend it to me? I'll pay you back in a couple weeks," Larry promised.

"Well—I'm saving to go on a fishing trip to Canada. But I still have three months. So—sure."

Larry signed the necessary papers, and they loaded the stereo into the car.

That evening, Larry invited all his friends to hear his new stereo. Owning something of top quality gave him a sense of importance. When he got paid, he went and bought six cassettes. Nick said he didn't need the money for a while, so Larry told himself there was no hurry.

A month went by and Nick mentioned the fact that Larry hadn't paid anything on the debt. "You said you didn't need the money until July," answered Larry. "I'll get it to you before then. Relax."

"But I'm losing the interest it could earn in my savings account," Nick protested.

"I'll pay you as soon as I get my next check," Larry promised.

But Larry owed his mother money and she put up such a fuss that

177

when payday came he forked over his whole check. This put him behind on his time payments with Radio Shack, so he had to make two payments the next month and pay a small penalty.

The relationship between Nick and Larry was becoming more and more strained. And the next time Nick mentioned the money he sounded angry.

Larry got defensive. "You don't understand. There was a big emergency and I had to give my mother the money."

"That's great—but what about me?" Nick fumed. "Without that $200 I won't be able to go on the fishing trip." With that, Nick turned his back and walked away.

Although Larry felt bad, it seemed as if he was helpless. There were things he wanted. Sure he felt a little guilty—but he carefully avoided Nick because from then on Larry couldn't bear to face his guilt.

Asking God to Meet Legitimate Needs

Dear God, I know you think I'm just great because you didn't make any inferior products. I don't need to buy expensive things to prove I'm worth something. Help me to live within my budget. I really could use more money than I have. Please give me a better job or show me some way I could earn some extra money. Help me budget better. I'll trust you for the money to _____ *and for a _____. But if that's not your will, I'll be content with what I have.*

📌 Getting the Facts Straight

The rich rule over the poor, and the borrower is servant to the lender. (Proverbs 22:7)

He will richly bless you, if only you fully obey the Lord your God and are careful to follow all these commands I am giving you today. For the Lord your God will bless you as He has promised, and you will lend to many nations but will borrow from none. (Deuteronomy 15:4–6)

Give everyone what you owe him: If you owe taxes, pay taxes; if revenue, then revenue; if respect, then respect; if honor, then honor. Let no debt remain outstanding, except the continuing debt to love one another. (Romans 13:7, 8)

The Bible is very clear on two things:
1. Being in debt is a curse, not a blessing.
2. Not paying your debts is sin.

Many believe that Christians should avoid debt completely. This point of view is expressed by Hudson Taylor, who was a highly respected missionary:

To me it seemed that the teaching of God's word was unmistakably clear: "Owe no man anything." To borrow money implied to my mind a contradiction of Scripture—a confession that God had withheld some good thing, and a determination to get for ourselves what He had not given.[1]

Because Deuteronomy 15:1–11 gives rules for handling debt among the Israelites and several verses in the Bible discuss lending money, others would not hold such a strict interpretation. Since being a borrower makes you a servant to the lender, however, you should try very hard to maintain your freedom. Being in debt has many dangers.

📌 Rethinking the Situation

It was an evening at the end of June, and Larry felt like having a sundae. He stopped at the Dairy Queen, and was surprised to see his

---

[1]Howard and Geraldine Taylor, *Hudson Taylor's Spiritual Secret* (Chicago: Moody Press, 1932), 81, 82.

friend Nancy working behind the counter. "I didn't know you worked here," he smiled. "I'll have to stop in more often."

But Nancy wasn't smiling. "I think you're a nerd," she blurted out. "Nick won't be able to go on his fishing trip unless you pay him back the money you owe him—and you don't even feel guilty."

"But you don't understand. I've had other important expenses—" Larry replied lamely.

"Everyone's talking about how you ripped off your best friend. If you were a friend at all, you'd take that stereo back to the store, or do something to pay back the money."

Larry walked out, blinking back the tears. The reason he'd bought the stereo in the first place was so his friends would consider him cool. Now he realized what people really thought of him. Worse yet, what did God think of him?

That night, he prayed to the Lord for forgiveness. The next week he sold his stereo.

When he gave the money to Nick, Larry felt happy and free. And he decided to kick the habit—the habit of buying things on credit.

✓ Putting the Truth Into Practice

Are you in debt? Are you a compulsive shopper? Do you buy things you really don't need?

1. Let God run your finances. Spend time praying before buying anything.

2. Seek the advice of a mature Christian who manages money well before making major purchases.

3. Learn self-control. Wait until you can pay cash for the things you buy.

4. Lower your standard of living until your debts are paid.

Overspending will destroy relationships, make you a slave and ruin your reputation.

CHAPTER 36

The Car That Cost Too Much

Brad left work at 9:30 P.M. Tuesday night and drove home as fast as he could. He still had to study for the big test *and* prepare an outline of his term paper. Working too many hours and under too much strain, Brad was beginning to hate school. He sensed a growing dislike for Ms. Bradshaw, who was really a very good teacher, because he thought she gave too much homework—like the big assignment that was due the next day. The one he hadn't touched yet!

At 12:30 Brad couldn't stay awake any longer, so he crawled into bed and set the alarm for 5:00 A.M.

He slept through the alarm—but his mother didn't. She stormed into his room. "Can't you show some consideration? I have enough trouble sleeping as it is, and I don't appreciate being awakened so early."

"Can't *you* understand?" Brad growled. "I thought that's what mothers are for! I had to work late and I'm exhausted. I have to finish my term-paper outline, or I get a zero. It's not *my* fault I slept through the alarm."

That got the day off to a miserable start. Brad felt as if he were on a treadmill. He *had* to work twenty-four hours a week to cover car payments, credit card debts and have some spending money. Thankfully, his ability with computers brought a good paycheck from the computer dealer where he worked.

His mind went back to August. When he'd started his senior year, Brad had wanted to make a good impression. The red Camero he wanted seemed worth the extra hours he'd have to work in order to afford it. Buying expensive clothes on credit seemed like the way to go. But now he had no time to enjoy his car. And he usually woke up late and threw on the first thing he saw.

Now Brad forced himself to concentrate on the term-paper outline. He concocted his main points more from guess work than from his little research. Then he dressed, downed some breakfast and drove off. But he wished he'd stayed in bed.

Colleen was waiting for him at his locker. "What's wrong?" she asked.

"Everything. I'm behind in my schoolwork. I'm totally exhausted, and I don't know what to do. If I'm going to pass English I guess I'll have to skip having dinner with you and skip youth group until I finish my term paper. It's the *only* time I have."

"But, Brad," Colleen complained, "I never get to see you. We might as well start sending each other letters. Maybe I should find a boyfriend who really cares about me."

The warning bell rang, and Colleen had to run to avoid being late for gym class. Dejected and discouraged, Brad walked into his first class and took his seat.

✔ Asking God to Meet Legitimate Needs

Dear God, show me how to use my money and my time in such a way as to glorify you. Keep me from buying things that would put me into financial bondage, robbing me of time with you and a peaceful and well-ordered life.

☛ Getting the Facts Straight

Do not wear yourself out to get rich; have the wisdom to show restraint. Cast but a glance at riches, and they are gone, for they will surely sprout wings and fly off to the sky like an eagle. (Proverbs 23:4, 5)

Better a little with fear of the Lord than great wealth with turmoil. Better a meal of vegetables where there is love than a fattened calf with hatred. (Proverbs 15:16, 17)

Better a dry crust with peace and quiet than a house full of feasting, with strife. (Proverbs 17:1)

The blessing of the Lord brings wealth, and he adds no trouble to it. (Proverbs 10:22)

It's true that God wants you to enjoy prosperity (*His* definition, not yours). But there are some warning signals that show you when your wants are out of line.

It isn't God's will that you wear yourself out, endanger your health and work too hard just to accumulate things or to put money in the bank. As we can see from Brad's predicament, living and working for material possessions is often accompanied by turmoil. It brings resentment and hatred directed against a person who seems to stand in the way of you enjoying your expensive lifestyle. It brings physical stress, and arguments with people you love. It adversely affects your spiritual life.

One pastor I knew said, "If you're too busy to go to prayer meeting, you're busier than God ever intended you to be."

If you're "rat racing" your way through life, find out what the root problem is. You'd be wise to lose interest in any wealth other than what comes from God's blessing. That's the only wealth you can be sure is trouble-free.

☛ Rethinking the Situation

Mechanically, Brad reached for a lunch tray, when a tap on the shoulder made him turn around.

It was Colleen. "I get to have lunch early today, because we're going to hear a special guest talk on Black history," she informed him.

When they found a place to sit down together, Colleen said, "I'm sorry about what I said earlier. I don't want another boyfriend. I want you. It's just that things can't go on like this. You work too hard, and you've forgotten how to enjoy life. And you're a *grouch.*"

"But what can I do?" Brad interrupted. "I have to pay for the car."

"*Sell* the car! Those monthly payments are causing this whole mess. Work eight hours on Saturday, get good grades—and take me to McDonald's!"

"But I can't sell the car!" he protested.

"Why not? Last spring when you walked and took buses, you came to school smiling."

Colleen was a real gem and Brad knew she was right.

Shortly, he did sell the car. Then he paid off his whole department store debt with his next paycheck.

After that, he began working only eight hours on Saturday. And he felt like a new person. The Tuesday night Bible studies were great. He got interested in his term paper and determined to do a top-notch job. He also helped his mother around the house—and he had more time to spend with Colleen!

He didn't even want to think what his life would still be like if he'd kept on working so much and making his car payments.

Putting the Truth Into Practice

Are you a slave to something—acquiring things, getting straight A's, having the perfect wardrobe, a 150 bowling average? *Relax.* If you've sacrificed keeping your mind on Jesus, sensible health habits, or integrity for your goal, something is radically wrong.

Stop trying to prove yourself. Fall into the arms of Jesus and receive all the affirmation and acceptance He has to give you. It's okay not to have the things your friends have, to get a lower grade now and then, to wear last year's coat and to throw a gutter ball. God, and your *real* friends, love you just the same.

CHAPTER 37

The Devastating Detour

Jason didn't really like his job at Taco Bell. The manager was always on his back, and he didn't make very much money. He felt like quitting. He couldn't understand Brent, who came to work smiling, did more than he was required to do, and seemed perfectly satisfied with his paycheck. But then, Brent was one of those "super-Christians." He read his Bible every day and even witnessed to his friends.

When Jason saw an ad in *Teen-Time Magazine* with the title, "How You Can Earn Over $20,000 a Year and Work Only Ten Hours a Week," he sent for information. He received a cassette catalog, order forms, receipt forms and a handbook on how to succeed as a "music man junior executive." He would get $3 for each order and $1.50 for each cassette sold by those he recruited to work under him. The road to riches meant picking an effective sales force.

Immediately Jason quit his job and started dreaming about what he'd do with $20,000 dollars. Because there was a "satisfaction guaranteed or your money back" promise and because the prices were much lower than retail stores, Jason collected a lot of orders. And he convinced quite a few friends to sell for him. When he asked Brent to become one of his salesmen, though, Brent replied, "Jason, most of the music on those cassettes is trash. How can you, as a Christian, sell that stuff with a clear conscience?"

"They'll buy it anyway," Jason countered. "And *I* might just as well make the money as someone else."

Some of Jason's sales people didn't keep good records, though, so he spent extra hours straightening things out before he sent in the orders.

When the cassettes arrived, they were inferior in quality and the company had taken the liberty to substitute when they were out of the number that had been requested. Over half the people who ordered wanted their money back. And Jason hadn't read the fine print that stated: "If the cassettes are returned, you pay the postage. If the cassettes sent back are postmarked later than a month after they were ordered, you are responsible for paying the money to the customer."

The next month was a nightmare. Jason borrowed money from his father to pay the postage. And because many packages were late, he received a bill from the company instead of a paycheck. Even worse, the kids at school were all disgusted with him.

On Sunday morning, he heard a sermon entitled "If Jesus Returned Today." Jason was beginning to feel very guilty for his part in helping teens obtain music that was ruining their lives. But he was still confused. How had this all happened? Didn't God promise prosperity?

THIS WAY OUT

✔ Asking God to Meet Legitimate Needs

Choose my instruction instead of silver, knowledge rather than choice gold, for wisdom is more precious than rubies, and nothing you desire can compare with her. I, wisdom, dwell together with prudence; I possess knowledge and discretion. . . . With me [wisdom] are riches and honor, enduring wealth and prosperity. . . . I walk in the way of righteousness, along the paths of justice, bestowing wealth on those who love me and making their treasuries full (Proverbs 8:10–12, 18, 20, 21)

Dear God, give me wisdom. Show me your ways. I know that prosperity is a byproduct of following your principles and receiving your council in all areas of my life.

🖍 Getting the Facts Straight

He who works his land will have abundant food, but one who chases fantasies will have his fill of poverty. A faithful man will be richly blessed, but one eager to get rich will not go unpunished. . . . A stingy man is eager to get rich and is unaware that poverty awaits him. (Proverbs 28:19, 20, 22)

Dishonest money dwindles away, but he who gathers money little by little makes it grow. (Proverbs 13:11)

He who works his land will have abundant food, but he who chases fantasies lacks judgment. (Proverbs 12:11)

An inheritance quickly gained at the beginning will not be blessed in the end. (Proverbs 20:21)

God does want to bless you, but He won't break the divine principles He's built into the universe to do it. God cannot lie. He won't change His mind in midstream. Certain actions receive His smile and others get His curse.

One of these unchangeables is that God has ordained that financial prosperity be the result of hard work and good planning. It's His will that we learn the art of money management so that we can live contentedly on the income we have. Get-rich-quick schemes are built on some catch—on deceptive advertising, on over-aggressive sales techniques, or on inferior products.

The book of Proverbs warns you against being eager to get rich. Wanting instant wealth implies either laziness, impatience, willingness to cheat a little to get it, or lack of trust in God. Jesus taught us to pray, "Give us this day our daily bread," not "Grant me a bank account so large that I never need to mention money to you again."

🖍 Rethinking the Situation

Brent noticed that Jason was eating lunch alone and that he looked super discouraged. He put his tray down across from him and sat down.

"Brent," Jason moaned, "I don't know what to do. I just got a bill from Classy Cassettes for $158. And I already owe my dad a bunch."

"Jason," Brent counseled, "your short-term problems can be easily solved by getting a job, working hard and not spending any money until you've paid back all the money you owe. But you need to deal with the root cause of this mess.

"The Bible condemns the person who's eager to get rich and who leaves a secure job to chase fantasies. It's dangerous to compromise your Christian principles just to make a fast buck."

"I guess what I did was really bad," Jason conceded. "I never knew that there was anything wrong with wanting to get rich quick. I thought God wanted Christians to prosper."

"He does," Brent responded, "but it only happens if we stick by the rules. It's not His will to bless you if you're making money vending something trashy. He won't help us if our method of selling violates the strict scriptural code of telling the truth. And He'll never put His mark of approval on laziness. If you're not diligent in the little things, God won't give you a lot."

"Well," Jason sighed, "you're worth listening to. Because you worked hard under that crabby manager at Taco Bell, you're a cashier at a better restaurant. You live your message. And really, I didn't know *all* that was in the Bible. I need to repent of selling that kind of music—and I better start reading the Bible every day just like you do."

🖊 Putting the Truth Into Practice

Decide to follow God's directions. Search out God's wisdom. Work hard at a sure and honest job. Get out of any work situation where lying, exaggerating, or deception is "required." Confess and forsake any desire to get rich quick. You obey God, and God gives the prosperity. Matthew 6:33 says, "But seek first his kingdom and his righteousness, and all these things will be given to you as well." That promise hasn't changed, and it never will.

CHAPTER 38

Making an Enemy to Love!

Crystal was a generally responsible and obedient person. Because of this, her mother trusted her. When she was elected to the National Honor Society, her mom beamed with pride. "Here's my Visa card," she said; "take it and buy a nice new outfit. I want you to feel confident when you give that speech in front of the whole school—and a new dress always helps."

Crystal headed for Ormonds. As she was looking through the rack of spring dresses, she felt a tap on the shoulder. It was Alicia, valedictorian of the senior class and the girl voted "Miss Popularity."

"What are you looking for?" she asked Crystal.

Flattered that Alicia took an interest in her, Crystal answered, "My mom's giving me a new dress for the National Honor Society installation. She let me take her Visa card."

"I wish I had parents like that," Alicia complained. "I'll be on the stage, too, with the rest of the people who were inducted last year. But I'll be wearing my old dress. And then there's still the senior banquet and the graduation tea. I wish I had folks like yours."

Still looking through the rack, Crystal spied the kind of dress she'd been looking for. The price was within reason. "What do you think of this one, Alicia?" she asked, holding it up.

"Ooh—nice! Why don't you try it on?"

When Crystal stepped out of the dressing room, she was delighted with what she had seen in the mirror.

Meanwhile, Alicia had found a suit that was especially stunning. They met at the three-way mirror outside the dressing rooms.

"Hey, you look great!" Alicia said.

"And you could go on TV with that outfit," Crystal replied.

"Crystal," Alicia begged, "couldn't you charge this on your mom's

189

card? I'll pay you back by the end of June. I already have a job with Parks and Recreation."

Crystal hesitated—but it was hard to turn down one of the most popular girls in school. And she felt sorry for her because she knew how much it meant to be well-dressed for the many senior activities. Being generous was something Crystal enjoyed. "Okay," she heard herself say, "but you must repay the money as soon as possible. My mom trusted me with this card."

Crystal made her purchase. When Alicia appeared with her suit, she suddenly blanched. "Oh no! I left my purse in the dressing room! Crystal could you please run and get it before someone steals it?"

"Sure," replied Crystal. But she looked all around the dressing room and couldn't find it anywhere.

When she finally returned Alicia was smiling. "What a goon I am! I put my purse in the bag with the yarn I bought for my mother. But thanks for looking."

She handed Crystal the Visa card, and they walked out with their packages.

At home Crystal told her mother what she'd done. She reimbursed her mom for the price of the suit, saying, "Alicia will pay me back, and I'll put that money in my college fund."

But on a Saturday morning two and a half weeks later, Crystal heard her mom let out a yell. The bill from Ormonds was nearly $500 more than the cost of the dress and the suit!

They called the store to double check, and it was then Crystal realized what had happened. While she was looking for the purse, Alicia had sneaked a bunch of other things to the clerk. By the time Crystal returned, the bill was already made up. She'd handed over the Visa card without paying attention to the extra charges.

☞ Asking God to Meet Legitimate Needs

Dear God, give me wisdom in my financial dealings. Show me the difference between generosity and foolishness, between showing mercy and throwing money away. You said we are to be "wise as serpents and harmless as doves." Give me wisdom for each situation.

☞ Getting the Facts Straight

A man lacking in judgment strikes hands in pledge and puts up security [promises to be responsible for another's debt] for his neighbor. (Proverbs 17:18)

Do not be a man who strikes hands in pledge or puts up security for debts; if you lack the means to pay, your very bed will be snatched from under you. (Proverbs 22:26, 27)

He who puts up security for another will surely suffer, but whoever refuses to strike hands in pledge is safe. (Proverbs 11:15)

My son, if you have put up security for your neighbor, if you have struck hands in pledge for another, if you have been trapped by what you said, ensnared by the words of your mouth, then do this, my son, to free yourself, since you have fallen into your neighbor's hands: Go and humble yourself; press your plea with your neighbor! Allow no sleep to your eyes, no slumber to your eyelids. Free yourself, like a gazelle from the hand of the hunter, like a bird from the snare of the fowler. (Proverbs 6:1-5)

Matthew Henry, a great Bible commentator, interprets these scriptures like this: "A man ought never to be bound as surety [signing to pay someone's debt such as consigning a bank note] for more than he is able and willing to pay and can afford to pay without wronging his family."[1] Based on Proverbs 22:26, I would add that you shouldn't lend money to help someone go into debt.

Jesus tells us, "Give to the one who asks you, and do not turn away from the one who wants to borrow from you." In Luke's account of the Sermon on the Mount, He further explains: "But love your enemies, do good to them, and lend to them without expecting to get anything back" (Luke 6:35). If you're willing to give away the money you lend (remember that God hates stinginess) and you seek God's wisdom before making a decision, you'll never face Crystal's problem.

☛ Rethinking the Situation

Now Crystal knew why Alicia kept avoiding her. Alicia wasn't a Christian and her ethical standards weren't based on biblical principles. Whenever she tried calling Alicia, somebody always said that she was out.

Crystal's mom shared with her some verses from Proverbs and she realized that by quickly lending money for the debt of a person she didn't know well, she had violated Scripture. Crystal resigned herself to the fact that she'd never see the money again. But she felt resentment against Alicia.

[1]Matthew Henry/Jamison/Fausset/Brown/Adam Clark/*The Bethany Parallel Commentary on the Old Testament* (Minneapolis: Bethany House Publishers, 1985), 121.

One day she read in her Bible, "Love your enemies." And she'd made an enemy to love! It even said, "Lend to them without expecting to get anything back!" And she knew she had to surrender her rights to God—her right to receive fair treatment, her right to the money she earned, and her right to the free time she'd lose by working extra hours to pay back her mother. She prayed, "Lord, I forgive Alicia. And I give my emotions, my money and my time to you."

Afterward she felt a real peace for the first time since she realized what Alicia had done.

Then she thought, "God, you're so great. Your Word not only tells us how to avoid problems in the first place, but how to escape from the ones we fall into."

✔ Putting the Truth Into Practice

Pray about your financial moves and get mature Christian advice. Crystal could have avoided her dilemma by simply saying, "I have to call my mother and see what she says." Wisdom and generosity go together. Ask God to give you both.

CHAPTER 39

Generation Get-Away

Dylan noticed the pretty dark-haired girl who showed up at their youth group. He made it a point to talk to her after the meeting. Jolene's southern drawl and her charm fascinated him. He offered her a ride home and invited her to a concert on Friday night. As he got to know Jolene, he realized that she was as beautiful on the inside as she was on the outside.

It was Christmastime when they met, and Dylan was busy selling gift boxes of chocolate candy that his friends could give as Christmas presents. Sales were great—until Rocky opened the candy he'd bought for his aunt and tasted it. He mouthed-off to the whole school that it was the worst candy he'd ever eaten. Dylan was swamped with demands for canceled orders and repayment of money.

He was mad at Rocky and didn't attempt to hide his feelings. On the way to visit Dylan's grandmother one day, he spouted off to Jolene. "If I were you," she replied, "I'd be glad Rocky sampled the chocolates. I certainly wouldn't want to be responsible for disappointing so many people. Did you eat any of the candy yourself?"

"No," Dylan said defensively.

"You should have," Jolene replied. "It's not good to sell inferior products."

"You don't understand," Dylan returned. "Rocky made me lose out on two or three hundred dollars!"

They rode on in uncomfortable silence until they reached Dylan's grandmother's house. She'd invited them for dinner and delicious smells met them as she opened the door.

Jolene and Dylan's grandmother took an immediate liking to each other. While Jolene listened and laughed, his grandmother shared some interesting stories of her youth and childhood.

Abruptly, Dylan changed the subject. "The neatest thing on the market is the Computer Chess Companion," he informed them. "I went over to Doug's house and he let me use his. It's a blast."

Jolene looked shocked, but remained silent. His grandmother took it all in stride and then resumed the childhood story she'd been telling.

On the way home, Jolene commented, "You sure sounded as if you were hinting to your grandmother for an expensive Christmas present."

"She's getting older, and she needs a little guidance. I'd hate to get something I couldn't use," Dylan replied.

Jolene seemed to be thinking for a time. Then she said, "You know I sponsor an orphan in the Philippines. I send her presents and everything. It's really neat to share with someone less fortunate, and it only costs $20 a month. Wouldn't you like to help some poor child?"

"I'd like to, but right now I can't afford it," Dylan lied.

"Sure you can," Jolene insisted. Turning on the overhead light, she fumbled in her purse for the information on sponsoring a child. Out tumbled the contents of her overstuffed handbag, including a bottle of nail polish. It hadn't been tightly closed and the lid came off, so polish ran all over the seat.

"Jolene!" Dylan shouted. "You ruined the upholstery!"

"I'm so sorry," Jolene apologized.

"Nail polish won't come off. You've just lowered the resale value of my car," Dylan accused.

Jolene said nothing. But she knew one thing: She'd never accept another date with a guy who was so self-centered and stingy.

☛ Asking God to Meet Legitimate Needs

Dear God, I trust you for the things I need and for those I want. Keep me from selfishness, greed and stinginess. Deliver me from the slavery of always worrying about my bank account, accumulating more possessions and conniving to get others to give me what I want. Free me to enjoy life and to put my confidence in you.

☛ Getting the Facts Straight

A greedy man brings trouble to his family, but he who hates bribes will live. (Proverbs 15:27)

A greedy man stirs up dissension, but he who trusts in the Lord will prosper. (Proverbs 28:25)

A stingy man is eager to get rich and is unaware that poverty awaits him. (Proverbs 28:22)

Do not eat the food of a stingy man, do not crave his delicacies; for he is the kind of man who is always thinking about the cost. (Proverbs 23:6, 7)

Greed is like a fatal disease—worse and worse symptoms start to manifest themselves. Unchecked selfishness creates trouble and dissention whenever it appears. You always feel uncomfortable around a stingy person.

The only cure is the one Jesus offered in Luke 9:23: "If anyone would come after me, he must deny himself and take up his cross daily and follow me" (Luke 9:23). He not only gives the correct instructions but He gives the power to fulfill them. Don't repeat the story of the rich young man who was so tied to his wealth that he couldn't part with it to serve Jesus. The words of Matthew 6:21— "where your treasure is, there your heart will be also"—suggest a great way to cure greed and selfishness. Invest liberally in God's work and pray for those ministries you support. Winning the world for Christ is much more exciting than watching your bank account or quantity of possessions grow.

☛ Rethinking the Situation

Dylan was used to squabbles with family and friends, so he didn't think much about the way he'd spoken to Jolene. When he called to ask for another date, her answer shocked him.

"Dylan," he heard on the other end of the line, "I can't date you anymore. You're so involved in yourself and your money that nothing else matters. Find a girl who thinks like you do, and you'll be happy."

With that, Jolene hung up.

Dylan was stunned. He honestly couldn't understand why Jolene was so offended. He decided to talk it over with the youth pastor.

After hearing Dylan's explanation, Pastor Dawson replied, "I've been watching you for three years. And to be honest, I've noticed that you really don't know how to be generous, or how to think of others before yourself. You always seem to think about money and possessions. It's like you're programmed to think, 'What's in it for me?' or 'How can I earn more money?' That's exactly the opposite of what Jesus taught."

He opened his Bible and read Luke 6:38: "Give, and it will be given to you. A good measure, pressed down, shaken together and running over, will be poured into your lap. For with the measure you use, it will be measured to you."

"I suggest that you do a Bible study on giving," he said. "And if you really want to change, I'll help you. I'll meet with you once a week."

Dylan knew his life needed transforming, so he accepted the challenge.

At least he knew where to start. He signed up to sponsor an orphan.

✔️ Putting the Truth Into Practice

Generosity Profile (Answer True or False)

_____ I get very upset if I lose some money or things don't go just my way.

_____ I have a hard time giving to church because there are too many things I want to buy for myself.

_____ I give broad hints and in other ways try to get people to pay my way or to give me things.

_____ If someone damages something I own I become very angry.

_____ I'm not too concerned about giving someone else a raw deal as long as I benefit.

_____ I rarely let my friend decide what he or she wants to do and refuse to participate in an activity I dislike just so my friend can be happy.

If you're guilty of any of these behaviors, ask God for forgiveness and receive His formula for change.

CHAPTER 40

Giving and Gaining

Donna attended an inner-city high school. Her father was on disability so they didn't have much to live on. He did make some extra money woodcarving, though, and her parents managed okay. She and her younger brothers and sisters were well-fed and provided with the necessities. Donna also worked after school so she could have spending money and buy a few nice things to wear. The result of all this was that she'd grown up despising lazy people who lived on welfare.

In spite of that, she and Shareen became friends. Shareen was a good student and Miss "Personality Plus." They sang together in the choir and in the girls' ensemble. Although they were together a lot at school, they never visited each other's homes. Shareen rarely talked about her family. About the only thing Donna knew was that Shareen's mother lived on public assistance and Shareen didn't know who her real father was.

The music teacher, Miss Mott, was famous for her spectacular choir concerts. After the girls' ensemble voted to buy pink blouses and long flowered skirts, Miss Mott arranged that the store order the extra outfits and put all of them on layaway. She announced that they were to pay for their clothes by April first, so they could be worn to dress rehearsal the Thursday before the big spring concert.

Three days before the deadline, Donna made her final payment. Proudly, she showed off her concert attire to her family.

The next day, Shareen came to school in tears. "My mother drank up all the money," she said despondently. "There's no way I can buy my blouse and skirt for the concert. Could you help me?"

"Shareen," Donna said, getting a little preachy, "you *know* how your mother is. You should have worked hard for the money, like *I* do. My parents can't afford any extras. I only have them because of my job." And all the while she was thinking that it would be too painful to part with the money she was saving to buy the new Reeboks she'd wanted for a long time.

Gina, a girl who hardly knew Shareen, came to her rescue and bought the outfit. Donna soon found out through the grapevine that Shareen and all the girls in the choir had decided that if all Christians were as stingy as Donna, they were better off *not* being Christians.

📝 Asking God to Meet Legitimate Needs

Dear God, help me to be unselfish and generous with my money, my time and my energy. Take away my prejudices. Give me YOUR wisdom and YOUR priorities.

📝 Getting the Facts Straight

One gives freely, yet gains even more; another withholds unduly, but comes to poverty. A generous man will prosper; he who refreshes others will himself be refreshed. People curse the man who hoards grain, but blessing crowns him who is willing to sell. (Proverbs 11:24–26)

He who oppresses the poor shows contempt for their Maker, but whoever is kind to the needy honors God. (Proverbs 14:31)

He who is kind to the poor lends to the Lord, and he will reward him for what he has done. (Proverbs 19:17)

He who despises his neighbor sins, but blessed is he who is kind to the needy. (Proverbs 14:21)

He who gives to the poor will lack nothing, but he who closes his eyes to them receives many curses. (Proverbs 28:27)

He who increases wealth by exorbitant interest amasses it for another, who will be kind to the poor. (Proverbs 28:8)

A good man leaves an inheritance for his children's children, but a sinner's wealth is stored up for the righteous. (Proverbs 13:22)

God wants to give money to people who will invest it wisely in His kingdom, financing God's work and helping the poor. You should be a channel through whom God can send money for good purposes. When you live to give, God will make sure that you get all the things you need, plus some special "extras" from time to time.

Sometimes it takes time for God's principle—putting money into the hands of those who obey Him—to take effect. Dedicated Christians often pass through times of financial stress. Great wealth can remain in the hands of sinners—sometimes for generations—but God says it's stored up for the righteous. Canaan was built up by the wicked to be given to God's people. Many Christian organizations now occupy property once owned by ungodly men who were forced to sell it cheap.

✔️ Rethinking the Situation

Donna came home from the dress rehearsal feeling condemned and discouraged. Passing the mirror she thought that she really did look good in her spring concert outfit—but even that failed to cheer her up. The devil seemed to be whispering, "You're a Scrooge, and you blew it."

Tears filled her eyes. She sat down with her Bible and opened it to 2 Corinthians 9. Phrases jumped out at her:

> Whoever sows sparingly will also reap sparingly, and whoever sows generously will also reap generously. (2 Corinthians 9:6)

> God loves a cheerful giver. (2 Corinthians 9:7)

> He has scattered abroad his gifts to the poor; his righteousness endures forever. (2 Corinthians 9:9)

All this reminded her of a verse she learned in second grade: "It is more blessed to give than to receive" (Acts 20:35).

She noticed that the Bible didn't say, "Give to the poor if they are responsible and deserving." It just said *give*. She asked God to forgive her attitude, and prayed for a second chance.

It came.

Shareen acted as mother to the younger children since her mother was rarely home. When she said that her little brother was broken-hearted because there was no money for a Little League baseball uniform, Donna offered to pay for it. Shareen looked surprised and expressed her gratitude over and over.

Donna even went with Shareen to watch Buster play. And when he hit a home run, she knew that she was really gaining by giving.

✔️ Putting the Truth Into Practice

Are you tight-fisted with your money? Have you sacrificed to give your parents something special? Are you willing to help people in need? If you live in a swanky suburb instead of in the inner city, that doesn't get you off the hook. You can give generously to whatever program your church has to help the poor. If you honestly don't know of an organization that aids the needy, ask your pastor or write to a Christian radio station for information.

Don't miss out on the blessings of generosity and sharing your wealth with those who have so little.

Self-Examination

Part IV: Dollars and Sense

FOR WHERE YOUR TREASURE IS
THERE WILL YOUR HEART BE
ALSO.

1. Giving to God one-tenth of all the money you receive is called _____.

2. "Godliness with c _____ is g _____" (1 Timothy 6:6).

3. Why is it wise to avoid debt?
   _____ a. The borrower is servant to the lender.
   _____ b. In the Bible being in debt is considered a curse.
   _____ c. The law of Moses forbade lending money.
   _____ d. Being in debt is often a sign that a person is discontent with what he or she has or can afford. Ingratitude is dangerous to spiritual health.

4. Are you wearing yourself out to acquire just the right clothes, to buy a car, or to have a lot of spending money? _____
   Is your spiritual life suffering because of it? _____
   What changes should you make? _____

5. Which of these things will keep God from blessing you?
   _____ a. Eagerness to get rich.
   _____ b. Making money on something that is less than honorable and honest.
   _____ c. Chasing fantasies.
   _____ d. Stinginess.

6. How can you add wisdom to your generosity?
   _____ a. Don't assume the responsibility of paying another's debt (unless you're willing and able to lose the money).
   _____ b. Lend without expecting the money to be returned.
   _____ c. If you've made a rash promise to give financial help, ask to be released.
   _____ d. Never say no to anyone.

7. Taking the biggest piece, always letting your friend pay, selling something for more than it's worth and worshiping a bank account are all signs of g _____ .

8. What does God promise the generous person?
   _____ a. Prosperity.
   _____ b. Rewards.
   _____ c. Supplying their needs so that they lack nothing.
   _____ d. Receiving refreshment from others.

9. Laziness is _____ .

10. What ridiculous excuse given by a lazy person is found in the book of Proverbs? _____

Answers: 1. Tithing; 2. Contentment, gain; 3. a, b, d; 4. Personal; 5. a, b, c, d; 6. a, b, c; 7. Greed; 8. a, b, c, d; 9. Sin; 10. "There's a lion in the streets."

Part Five

The Terrible Trio: Pride, Rash Actions, Revenge

CHAPTER 41

The Problem Called Pride

Travis looked at the florescent dial on his watch. It was midnight. Because of the burning pain in his right leg, he couldn't get to sleep. Although he pushed his button to call a nurse, no one came. All the commotion in the room across the hall indicated that the emergency there would keep the hospital staff occupied for some time. From his hospital bed he relived the last two days.

Although it seemed like ages ago, it was only yesterday that he had been voted Outstanding Student of Meadowbrook Junior High. Thunderous applause had greeted him when the announcement was made at an assembly. Travis was called to the stage, and as the principal shook his hand a local newspaperman took several pictures. When the three o'clock bell rang, his friends mobbed him. Being a celebrity was great!

He had dreamed about being chosen Outstanding Student of the Nation and shaking hands with the President. As he was dressing for school, an inner voice seemed to whisper, "You're really something. Straight-A student. More RBI's than any other player in the league. Winner of the 'What America Means to Me' speech contest—and not bad to look at in the mirror."

Whisking a comb through his hair, Travis turned his thoughts to his other triumphs. He was popular with the girls, a better than average guitar player, and if he kept learning more stunts on his unicycle he might just have to turn down a chance to join the circus.

It was then his mother called the family to breakfast. But before Travis sat down, he noticed his little brother's report card on the counter.

"Tyler," he teased, "how could you get a C– in *spelling*? That's pretty dumb. And if you don't lose some weight, you'll never be a good baseball player."

207

"Travis," his father interrupted, "don't let your accomplishments go to your head. Pride can be dangerous, you know."

But Travis wasn't really listening. Mechanically, he said grace with the rest of the family, and reached for the plate of pancakes in the middle of the table.

"Whatever happened to 'ladies first'?" his ten-year-old sister, Tanya, wanted to know.

"Survival of the fittest," quipped Travis as he forked four big pancakes onto his plate.

Throughout the day, he received congratulations from everybody. He felt more important than ever before.

When his sixth-hour history teacher asked, "Who won the election of 1902?" Travis was the only student with an answer: "Teddy Roosevelt."

"You're wrong," the teacher announced.

"No, I'm not," Travis shot back. "Teddy Roosevelt was president in 1903 when the Wright brothers flew their first airplane. I just read it in *The History of Aviation* and I'll show it to you."

"You're wrong," the teacher said triumphantly, "because there was no election in 1902."

Everybody laughed, and Travis felt his face turn red. As he walked out of class, he decided that he *had* to regain his loss of face somehow.

After baseball practice, the unicycle group met to shape up their act for the annual Meadowbrook Junior High Carnival. They were still waiting for Bill when Travis began to show off a little. But a moment later, his stunt hurled him onto the cement.

Excruciating pain shot through his body. After that he blanked out and the next thing he knew, he was being carried into the emergency room.

Why did this have to happen, he thought angrily, *just before the championship game?* He wouldn't even get to go on the eighth-grade picnic.

A verse he learned in Sunday school kept coming back to him: "Pride goes before destruction, a haughty spirit before a fall" (Proverbs 16:18).

🖋 Asking God to Meet Legitimate Needs

There's a difference between feeling good about yourself as you completely depend on God, and being conceited.

True humility isn't saying "I'm not good," or "I never do anything right." It's affirming that "I can do everything *through him who gives me strength*" (Philippians 4:13). It's cooperating with God and enjoying what you do.

Dear God, help me to form a partnership with you in developing my personality and planning my life, so that I realize my true potential and experience a sense of fulfillment in all I do. Keep me from the self-sufficiency that results in ugly pride.

🖋 Rethinking the Situation

The next day, Travis was wheeled to the operating room. After surgery, they put his leg in traction. He was told that he'd be confined to his hospital bed until they were sure that the bones were healing properly.

Always the first to finish, the top of his group, and the kid who others admired, Travis now struggled just to take a drink of water. Helpless to do anything for himself, Travis realized that he was dependent on God for every breath.

He thanked God for the brains He had given him and determined to use them for His glory. If he'd landed on his head, maybe he wouldn't even know who was president of the United States *today*! He became grateful for his athletic talent and realized he had better not take it for granted. Now he could put himself in the place of those with less ability, and he realized that his pride had hurt others. He wrote a letter to his history teacher, apologizing for his arrogant attitude.

When Tyler came for a visit, Travis asked forgiveness for always acting superior. He even told Tanya that he was sorry for habitually grabbing the food first.

Meadowbrook Junior High baseball team won the championship. That was when Travis really learned that the world ran very well without him!

And when his youth pastor came for a visit, he left something for Travis to think about: "God's given you tremendous ability—but He only uses people who are humble enough to realize they need Him every minute. *If you surrender totally to God and rely on His power,* there's no limit to what you can do for Him."

✔ Getting the Facts Straight

On the appointed day Herod, wearing his royal robes, sat on his throne and delivered a public address to the people. They shouted, "This is the voice of god, not of a man." Immediately, because Herod did not give praise to God, an angel of the Lord struck him down, and he was eaten by worms and died. (Acts 12:21–23)

Herod's problem wasn't that he had authority and talent recognized by other people. It was that he didn't give God the credit. Humility isn't saying that you're ugly, that you're a klutz or that you don't have a brain in your head. It's thanking God for your good looks, your athletic ability and your intelligence. It's recognizing that God gave you all the talent you possess and using it for His glory.

When pride comes, then comes disgrace, but with humility comes wisdom. (Proverbs 11:2)

The Lord detests all the proud of heart. Be sure of this: They will not go unpunished. (Proverbs 16:5)

Before his downfall a man's heart is proud, but humility comes before honor. (Proverbs 18:12)

A man's pride brings him low, but a man of lowly spirit gains honor. (Proverbs 29:23)

The pride that forgets God and shows off will always be punished. Sometimes the consequences will be a lot more subtle than those that Travis experienced. Perhaps the downfall won't come for a long time, but it will come. For that reason Matthew Henry advises us not to be worried when we see pride in others, but to greatly fear it in ourselves.

Putting the Truth Into Practice

Decide to learn how to always give God the glory for each victory. Never forget that without the breath, intelligence, talent and energy *He* gives you, *nothing* could be accomplished.

When you're tempted to take all the credit, *don't.* Instead of being the star of your own show, give the microphone—or the football, or the trumpet—to Jesus. Let Him shine through you.

CHAPTER 42

Pity-Party Blueprint

Brian was discouraged, angry—and totally unaware of the big "chip" he carried on his shoulder.

As always, nothing seemed to be going right. He thought that his teachers picked on him, that his father paid more attention to his younger brother, and that his aunt forgot his birthday on purpose. He was upset because the kids at church hadn't made a big deal over missing him the Sunday he was home with the flu. Although he stomped into the principal's office to complain, the students still called him wimpy in gym class. On top of everything, Clark, his best friend, had walked by him in the hall one day and didn't even say "hi."

Mr. Whitener, the counselor at his school, was a Christian and attended Brian's church. One afternoon, Brian was called into the counselor's office. That was a switch. Usually, Brian was the one who made the appointments so that he could complain to someone about his grades, or the unfair treatment he was getting from one teacher or another.

"Brian," Mr. Whitener began, "I've been watching you lately and I've noticed how miserable you are. I want to help you, and I have some advice I hope you'll consider. What I have to say is going to be hard to hear, though.

"Your pride and self-centeredness are making you unhappy. Every time someone fails to notice you, or when things don't go your way, you explode. You don't consider the feelings of others. You don't give anyone the benefit of the doubt. You assume that everyone is out to get you just because they don't react the way *you* think they should."

"You don't understand me!" Brian responded angrily. "You're just having a bad day, so you're taking all your frustration out on me."

"Brian, please listen to what I'm saying," Mr. Whitener countered. "Hear me out.

"First of all, if you get a bad grade, don't blame the teacher. Just study harder for the next test. Always be friendly—whether or not the other person responds. Sometimes people are preoccupied with their own problems, and they're unaware of their surroundings. Stop comparing yourself with others and becoming jealous when they get things you're unable to have. And relax! Take a little teasing—it's part of life."

"Do you expect me to be a doormat?" Brian flared. "I don't like being pushed around by everyone, and I'm *not* going to take it."

"Brian, please listen to what God has to say on the subject."

Taking his Bible from his desk, Mr. Whitener read:

> You have heard that it was said, "Eye for eye, and tooth for tooth." But I tell you, Do not resist an evil person. If someone strikes you on the right cheek, turn to him the other also. . . . Love your enemies and pray for those who persecute you. (Matthew 5:38, 39, 44)

"I don't need your sermon," Brian spouted. With that, he walked out and slammed the door.

☑ Asking God to Meet Legitimate Needs

Dear God, forgive my pride. Give me the love and acceptance I need so I won't expect too much from other people. Keep me from being the center of my own universe and expecting everything to revolve around me. Help me not to be oversensitive and demanding of attention.

✔ Getting the Facts Straight

Because pride is totally self-centered, the arrogant person constantly has hurt feelings. Pride creates quarrels and dissention. Pride looks down on others and refuses to take advice. The conceited person forgets God and shuns anyone who doesn't fit into his or her scheme of things.

> Pride only breeds quarrels, but wisdom is found in those who take advice. (Proverbs 13:10)

> Haughty eyes and a proud heart, the lamp of the wicked, are sin! (Proverbs 21:4)

> The proud and arrogant man—"Mocker" is his name; he behaves with overweening pride. (Proverbs 21:24)

✔ Rethinking the Situation

When Brian realized that every guy on the tennis team had been invited to Sheldon's birthday party except "Dennis the Menace" (the most disliked kid at school) and him, he decided that he had to do something about his life.

Mr. Whitener's words came back to him: "Your pride and self-centeredness are making you unhappy." He had to admit that this was true.

When he thought about it, he realized that his response to the Bible passages Mr. Whitener read amounted to talking back to God. The card his mother had put on his desk had this verse on it:

> Do not be quick with your mouth, do not be hasty in your heart to utter anything before God. God is in heaven and you are on earth, so let your words be few. (Ecclesiastes 5:2)

He felt as if God had written it especially for him—and that was a humbling experience. He *had* to change and he knew a good place to start. He'd been daydreaming in math class all week and hadn't cracked the book. He already knew what his grade on Friday's test would be.

When Mr. Madison passed out the exams and Brian's paper was returned to him with an *F*, he held his temper. Instead of blowing up, he went up to the teacher after class and admitted, "I deserved this grade." He even accepted extra homework, wrote down the assignment and hurried to his locker to pick up his other books.

✍ Putting the Truth Into Practice

1. List the times you reacted when your feelings were hurt. How did your pride play a part in what happened?

2. When have you said, "I don't need anyone telling me what to do?" Or when have you refused, in direct or indirect ways, to listen to advice?

Decide that you'll forgive insults and not expect to be the center of attention. Listen seriously to the counsel of others. "Those that are humble and peaceable will ask and take advice, will consult their own consciences, their Bibles, their ministers, their friends to preserve quietness and prevent quarrels."[1] Determine to join their ranks. Matthew Henry also affirms that pride makes God your enemy and the devil your master.

Don't let the poison of pride ruin your life.

[1]Matthew Henry/Jamison/Fausset/Brown/Adam Clark/*The Bethany Parallel Commentary on the Old Testament* (Minneapolis: Bethany House Publishers, 1985), 1231.

CHAPTER 43

Who Do You Think You Are?

Rafael was born in Mexico. When he was two years old, his parents had moved to California. The oldest of eight, he'd had to work hard and was often left in charge of the other children.

School was the bright spot in Rafael's life. He got good grades and excelled in athletics. Through a program to help minority kids, he was given a trumpet and a chance to play in the band. He practiced hard and learned fast.

He was ashamed, though, of his poor home and junky yard. His parents didn't catch on to American ways or learn much English. He determined that he would be different. He'd make something of his life.

In his sophomore year, a friend at school witnessed to him and Rafael accepted Christ as his Savior. He joined the Christian club at their high school and became active in a local church. By working long hours each summer and after school, he managed to save enough money to buy a respectable-looking car and to dress well. No one suspected the kind of home he came from.

As a senior, Rafael was named to the national honor society, played first-chair trumpet in the band, and was a star baseball player. He was *very* popular.

When he asked Amber for a date that November she enthusiastically accepted. Driving up to her gorgeous home, Rafael realized how different their backgrounds were. Her father was a college graduate and a bank president. Rafael didn't want to spoil things by letting Amber know what his family was like.

Their relationship moved quickly, and Rafael decided he was really "in love." The best part was that Amber seemed to feel exactly the same way about him.

Early in the spring, Amber and her family left for a weekend, and when her family returned she stayed a couple of extra days with her girlfriend. It was arranged that Rafael would pick her up at the bus depot.

Rafael watched as people got off the bus and soon he spotted Amber's smiling face.

As he picked up her suitcase, he nearly did a double-take. There were his poorly dressed uncle and cousin, claiming the battered box they'd brought with them from Mexico!

He turned away and hoped they hadn't seen him. But it was too late.

"Rafa!" yelled his uncle.

Instead of stopping, Rafael grabbed Amber's arm and pushed her rapidly toward the parking lot. "What's the big rush?" Amber wanted to know. "We *could* walk a little slower."

Just then Rafael's cousin caught up with them. He was talking fast, in broken English. "Rafael! Why you walk away when we call to you?"

Amber turned to him. "You turned your back on them, didn't you? On your own relatives. Who do you think you are? If you don't take them with you, I'm not going."

The four of them rode together in complete silence. When Rafael dropped Amber off at her house, she didn't even say "thank you."

THIS WAY OUT →

☛ Asking God to Meet Legitimate Needs

You need to accept yourself just the way you are, with all the *unchangeables*—your physical appearance, family background and mental ability. The pride that makes you pretend to be somebody you're not is a sin. It hurts you *and* others. Failure to see that God has a purpose for each unchangeable feature of your life—and those of other people—will result in the pride that covers something up or looks down on another.

Dear God, help me to accept what I cannot change—my family, my home and the way you made me. Since you created each person, show me how to love and accept everybody.

☛ Getting the Facts Straight

There are six things the Lord hates, seven that are detestable to him. [And the first one on the list is "haughty eyes."] (Proverbs 6:16)

Haughty eyes and a proud heart, the lamp of the wicked, are sin. (Proverbs 21:4)

Do not be proud, but be willing to associate with people of low position. Do not be conceited. (Romans 12:16)

That stuck-up glance says, "I can't stand you." Looking down on others is a sin that God detests.

☛ Rethinking the Situation

Rafael knew that Amber had a right to be disappointed with him.
Arriving at the house, the three filed silenty into the living room. When he saw the wounded look on his uncle's face, Rafael began to cry. Finally, Rafael recovered enough to apologize.

After his father got home from work, Rafael confessed everything to his dad and asked forgiveness for being ashamed of his family. He thanked his father for everything he'd done for him.

For the first time since he was a little boy, Rafael told his father he loved and admired him. As they both cried and embraced each other, he felt as if a tremendous burden had lifted from his shoulders.

And for the first time in his life, he realized that he had reason to be proud of his family.

✔ Putting the Truth Into Practice

Is there someone you don't want to be seen with? Is it the not-so-cool kid from church, or the fat girl at school? Do you consider yourself too good for some people? Are you ashamed of your family, or something in your background?

1. Ask God to make you so secure in Him that you don't have to manufacture a sense of worth from the people you're seen with or your social status.

2. Confess the sin of looking down on other people.

3. Do something special for the person you'd rather not associate with.

CHAPTER 44

The Leap-Before-You-Look Labyrinth

Aaron came back from the youth retreat all fired up. He'd vowed that winning his school for Christ would be his top priority.

There had to be some way that every kid in school could hear the Gospel. Witnessing to each person individually seemed impossible. Then, Aaron got an idea!

As a member of the Student Council, he was on the assembly committee. A friend had told him about an ex-drug addict who gave school assemblies on "substance abuse"—and at the same time wove in his Christian testimony.

Aaron wrote to the man and received a positive reply. Since the principal, Mr. Black, was especially interested in this problem he gave his consent.

All the Christians in the school were excited about the assembly. Aaron had arranged to meet the speaker on stage a half hour before the program was to begin. But the students were in their seats and Mr. Black was already making introductory remarks when the speaker arrived.

When the speaker stood up, Aaron was surprised to see an older gentleman dressed in a suit and tie and carrying a two-ton Bible! He walked to the lectern, and after a few trite comments about chemical dependency, he launched into a hell-fire and brimstone sermon! Within ten minutes, the students had booed him off the stage and they were sent back to their classes.

Mr. Black called Aaron to his office. "Do you realize that you not only deceived me, but you broke the law of the land? That guy was a fake. He didn't know anything about drug use. And I could get into trouble for authorizing a religious assembly. I'll get angry calls from parents. I'll be blamed for something that's all your fault! Aaron, I thought you were honest. How could you do such a thing? I lose all respect for fanatics who don't live their Christianity."

Dazed and shaken, Aaron walked out into the hall. How could such good intentions produce such a disaster? What went wrong?

THIS WAY OUT →

☞ Asking God to Meet Legitimate Needs

Jesus said, "Go into all the world and preach the good news to all creation" (Mark 16:15). Finding ways to share your faith is a basic necessity of your Christian life.

But don't do it your way. Ask God for *His* methods. And don't be so afraid of making mistakes that you disobey His command to "go and make disciples of all nations" (Matthew 28:19).

Dear God, I pray for _____ and _____ .
Show me how I can best witness to each one. Show us Christians
your strategy for reaching our school.

☞ Getting the Facts Straight

It is not good to have zeal without knowledge, nor to be hasty and miss the way. (Proverbs 19:2)

A discerning man keeps wisdom in view, but a fool's eyes wander to the ends of the earth. (Proverbs 17:24)

222

Aaron made several mistakes:

1. He didn't do a lot of praying before acting.
2. He didn't receive advice from mature Christians.
3. He entrusted a very important job to someone without carefully checking that person's qualifications, integrity and ability to handle the situation.
4. He thought in terms of short-range goals rather than concentrating on long-haul results.

☑ Rethinking the Situation

On his way home, Aaron went to see his youth pastor. When Pastor Bob heard what happened, he said, "You need someone to talk to. Let's go out for a Coke."

As they talked, Pastor Bob suggested that Aaron go to Mr. Black and explain what had happened. "Maybe you should also offer to talk personally with any parents who complain."

Aaron took his advice. And Mr. Black was impressed when he apologized.

After a lot of praying and some advice from older Christians, the kids in Aaron's group decided to have an evangelistic Valentine party. Jessie would give out all the invitations since the party would be at his home. So students would know what kind of party it was and no deception would be involved, the invitation clearly stated: "There will be a short talk on 'Discovering Real Love in Jesus.' "

A lot of new kids came to the party. And three of them accepted Jesus as Savior that night!

Judy offered to have the next evangelistic party at her house. And Aaron was happy to see that God was at work in spite of the mistake he'd made.

☑ Putting the Truth Into Practice

Enthusiasm is wonderful, but it must be properly channeled. Sometimes the young person's frustration with stodgy, negative adults makes him or her want to blast ahead regardless of caution and common sense. Others just aren't disciplined enough for careful planning, seeking advice and attending to details. But if you carefully assimilate the teachings of Proverbs, you can keep all your enthusiasm and still act wisely.

What are you currently excited about doing? Evangelizing in the inner city? Taking a long bike trip? Getting a job in a national park?

Before you act, reread the four mistakes that Aaron made and write down how you can avoid falling into the same trap.

CHAPTER 45

The Bargain

John had dreamed for so long of having a car of his own. Wheels spelled independence and freedom. He'd been carefully saving his money, and his parents had at last given him permission to buy a car.

Ecstatic, John took a bus to the biggest used car lot in the city. As he looked at the prices, he became more and more dismayed. The $1000 he'd saved wouldn't buy anything.

A gray-haired man approached him. "Sonny," he began, laying a hand on his shoulder, "I can see that you really want a car. But my guess is, these are too expensive for you.

"I have a beautiful car in my garage and I'll sell it to you for $500. It's worth a lot more, but I remember what it was like to be young and to want a car I couldn't afford."

It seemed too good to be true! John hopped into the man's automobile and they drove to his home. The red car in the garage had a perfect paint job, impeccable black vinyl seat covers and almost-new tires. Obviously, it had been driven very little.

John's face brightened. "Can I take it for a drive?"

"Not right now," the man said. "It needs a couple minor repairs. If you give me the money, I'll have the car ready for you Monday at 5:00 P.M."

Impulsively, John handed him $500 in cash, took down his address and phone number, and left elated.

He decided to keep the car a secret so he could surprise everybody. But for the rest of the week he could think of nothing else.

Monday at 4:30, John was in front of the elderly man's house. He saw the car in the driveway, but decided to wait until 5:00 before knocking at the door. The man smiled, gave him the keys and went back inside.

When he turned the ignition key, the engine choked and sputtered. Finally, John knocked on the door again. "The car won't start," he fumed.

"Take it easy," the man soothed. "I haven't driven it for ten years so it needs to warm up. After a couple hundred miles, it'll run like a rabbit."

John tried again and finally got the thing going. It jerked and coughed all the way home. At one intersection the engine died, and the light changed three times before he got started again.

His father was just getting home from work when John drove into the driveway. Taking one look at the car, his father moaned, "How could you?"

"What's the matter?" John asked.

"This car was discontinued *years* ago. There's no place to get parts for it. Why didn't you ask my advice? Why didn't you study up on different models and book prices? You just threw your money away."

THIS WAY OUT ➤

📌 Asking God to Meet Legitimate Needs

You must learn how to take the time to make sensible decisions. The devil specializes in provoking rash action because he loves to see people suffer.

Dear God, help me avoid jumping to conclusions without having all the facts, for acting without knowledge or advice. Please give me the discernment and the prudence I need to make wise decisions.

🖝 Getting the Facts Straight

Every prudent man acts out of knowledge, but a fool exposes his folly. (Proverbs 13:16)

The wisdom of the prudent is to give thought to their ways, but the folly of fools is deception. (Proverbs 14:8)

A simple man believes anything, but a prudent man gives thought to his steps. (Proverbs 14:15)

The heart of the discerning acquires knowledge; the ears of the wise seek it out. (Proverbs 18:15)

If you make rash decisions, you are disregarding God's Word. If you act without first gaining the advice and knowledge that will enable you to choose wisely, you're asking for trouble. Even if you feel God has directed you to say or do something special or unusual, it's almost always advisable to ask Him for confirmation over a period of time before rushing into action.

🖝 Rethinking the Situation

A year later, after saving up more money, John was ready to buy his first car. This time he went to the public library to check *Consumer Reports* magazine, and he invited his father and a friend who had studied auto mechanics to help him make the purchase.

He was attracted by a used but flashy-looking old Mustang, with an immaculate interior. But when his father and friend cautioned him, explaining that the engine needed too many repairs, John listened. The less impressive vehicle he ended up buying proved to be reliable and economical transportation.

🖝 Putting the Truth Into Practice

List the decisions you've made recently—buying a new coat, signing up for drama, applying for work at Burger King, etc. Ask yourself the following questions.
1. Did you seriously pray about it?
2. How many people (preferably mature Christians) did you ask for advice?

3. What questions did you get answered before acting?
   Examples of investigating and questioning:
   - What fabrics are most durable? What colors are most practical? Which store has the best price?
   - Did you ask your school counselor what courses you'll need for your chosen career? Did you find out if the dramas to be presented are in line with your conscience as a Christian?
   - Did you interview someone who works at Burger King to find out what the place is like? Did you ask what hours you'd be working to make sure they wouldn't conflict with church and Bible study, etc.?

   Next list future decisions you must make.
   1. Start praying now.
   2. Whose advice do you plan to seek?
   3. What questions do you need to find answers to in order to choose wisely?

Take the World off Your Shoulders

In Hillary's family, getting even was a game everybody played.

When her father lost a substantial amount of money playing poker, for instance, her mother went out and bought a lot of expensive clothes and charged them on his credit card. Her father then stopped speaking to her mother—until she couldn't stand it anymore, apologized, and agreed to take some of the clothes back to the store.

Sometimes things got completely out of hand. When Hillary borrowed her brother's car without asking and had an accident, he told her boyfriend that she was secretly dating another guy and her boyfriend broke up with her. Hillary got so angry that she "accidentally" broke his CD player.

At the same time, Hillary had noticed that Tara and her family were completely different.

When Tara tried out for cheerleading, her performance was obviously better than the other candidates. The returning members of the squad all voted against her, though, because Andrea, their self-appointed leader, hated Christians. And Tara wasn't even angry!

She said, "God doesn't make mistakes. So I know He has a *good* reason for allowing this to happen." She even told Hillary that she was praying for Andrea.

To top it off, a month later, when Andrea broke her leg and ended up in the hospital, Tara brought her a little gift.

Hillary couldn't believe what she saw. "What is it about you?"

Tara explained the Gospel to her, then asked, "Do you want to invite Jesus into your heart, Hillary?"

Hillary did ask Christ to be her Savior. And in short order, God started making changes in her life.

Not everything changed, though. Hillary had assumed that now she'd automatically love everyone. But it wasn't quite that easy.

One night Hillary's parents entertained special company. She volunteered to clear the table, clean up the kitchen and load the dishwasher. Without thinking, she put an antique porcelain plate made in 1869 in with the others. During the wash cycle, it broke into little pieces.

Besides a fifteen-minute volcanic verbal explosion, Hillary's mother grounded her daughter every Friday and Saturday night until the end of the semester.

Hillary was furious. She hadn't done anything wrong on purpose. Besides, she had just started dating Christopher and eleven lost weekends was enough to kill any romance!

Without thinking twice, Hillary took her usual course of action. She drove over to her grandmother's house in tears. Explaining how unjust her mother's punishment was, she expected her grandmother to take her side.

But it backfired. Her grandmother flew into a rage. "*Just* a broken plate!" she screamed. "That plate was the only family heirloom we had from the old country. It survived the war. And it was the only valuable thing I brought with me when I came to America. It was the only remembrance I had of my mother and my grandmother. How could you be so thoughtless?"

THIS WAY OUT

✔ Asking God to Meet Legitimate Needs

Dear God, I know that turn-the-other-cheek love only comes from you, and I desperately need some. I receive it from you by faith. You know that right now I'm being tempted to get even with _____ for _____ . I know that taking revenge is sin. I'll leave the job of punishing the wicked to you. Forgive me for trying to be God.

✔ Getting the Facts Straight

If a man digs a pit, he will fall into it; if a man rolls a stone, it will roll back on him. (Proverbs 26:27)

Do not say, "I'll pay you back for this wrong!" Wait for the Lord and he will deliver you. (Proverbs 20:22)

Do not say, "I'll do to him as he has done to me; I'll pay that man back for what he did." (Proverbs 24:29)

When you've been wronged, the temptation to get even is very strong.

Let David's manner of handling Saul be a model for you when you're tempted to take revenge for some injustice. Saul was mentally deranged, and took his whole army to try to kill David just because he did everything right and the people loved him! David, on the other hand, never arranged to overthrow the government so he could be king as God had promised. He did not take justice into his own hands. He let God do it His way—which always seems to be a lot slower than ours. In some of his prayers, as recorded in the Psalms, David does have some suggestions for God on how to punish his enemies. But he himself does nothing.

When you're unfairly treated, ask God to take up your case—and follow His command to love those who persecute you.

✔ Rethinking the Situation

The next morning before school, Hillary told Tara the whole story. Tara was understanding, but firm.

"Hillary," she began, "you have to learn to let God be God. The One who controls the whole universe can run your life better than you can. Romans 12:19 says, 'Do not take revenge, my friends, but leave room for God's wrath, for it is written: It is mine to avenge; I will repay, says the Lord.' That's a good Bible verse for you to learn and put into practice.

"Sure, technically it's unfair for you to be punished for doing what you thought was a good deed. But maybe God wants to use this to break your habit of always trying to get even. You're worried that losing your usual date night will make Christopher look for another girl. But you need to give your relationship with Christopher to God. If it's God's will that you and Christopher remain together things will work out, even if he and his family move to China!

"Another thing. You'll never clear up this whole mess unless you confess to your brother that you broke his CD player. And if he retaliates, let God defend you. No matter what happens, don't try to get back at him. Let God run your life."

✔ Putting the Truth Into Practice

List your habits of revenge. (Like, making your parents feel guilty if you don't get your own way; deciding not to speak to the person you're mad at; doing certain things on purpose to rile a teacher.)

_____

_____

_____

_____

_____

Over each one, in a different color ink, write these words: "Do not say, 'I'll pay you back for this wrong!' Wait for the Lord, and he will deliver you."

Is Satan tempting you right now to get back at someone? Decide to obey God. Do a lot of praying. And stop planning your attack!

CHAPTER 47

Return to the "Plain Jane Club"

Shauna, Mallory, Lacie and Felicia always ate lunch together at school. They listened to each other, stuck up for each other, played on the same intramural volleyball team and attended meetings of the Christian club in their school. They had a lot in common: They got good grades, they were "good girl" types—and they had trouble landing dates.

Sometimes Mallory would despair. "I guess we're just members of the 'Plain Jane Club.' " Although no one especially liked the name, it stuck.

When Shauna was asked out by Jeremy, the captain of the football team, there was instant rejoicing. The "Plain Jane Club" was sending a representative to "Popularity Pedestal"! Only Lacie had the presence of mind to warn Shauna against dating a non-Christian.

Shauna's rise as a socialite soon caused problems in the group. At first she did nothing but brag about her dates with Jeremy. Soon she was hanging around with the "popular" crowd, and hardly spoke to her old friends anymore.

Mallory's birthday party was dinner in a nice restaurant with the "Plain Jane Club." Even though Shauna had shunned her, Mallory felt that as a Christian she should invite her anyway.

When Shauna walked in she was wearing a knock-out party dress. Her description of the dinner party she was attending with Jeremy that night dominated the conversation. After eating just an appetizer, she excused herself, explaining that she needed to re-do her hair, which hadn't turned out just right. Mallory was deeply hurt.

When Shauna's birthday rolled around, she didn't invite any of her old friends to her party.

Then one day it happened. The news flash from the grapevine

reached the entire school before lunch: Jeremy had dumped Shauna.

"Serves her right," Mallory told Lacie and Felicia with a triumphant grin. "Maybe now she'll know how it feels."

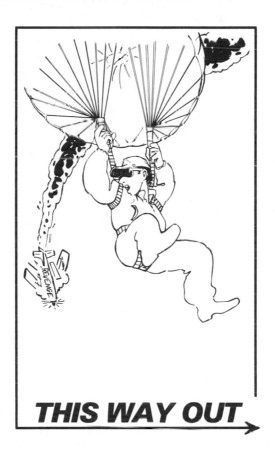

THIS WAY OUT

📌 Asking God to Meet Legitimate Needs

Dear God, I know it's not right to rejoice at someone else's misfortune—so keep me from having a judgmental attitude. Give me your love for people who don't deserve it. Help me to remember that your love never changes and that it's there no matter what I've done. As your child, I'm supposed to act like you and love unconditionally. Show me how to receive that kind of love from you, and how to pass it on.

🖎 Getting the Facts Straight

> Do not gloat when your enemy falls; when he stumbles, do not let your heart rejoice, or the Lord will see and disapprove and turn his wrath away from him. (Proverbs 24:17, 18)

> He who mocks the poor shows contempt for their Maker; whoever gloats over disaster will not go unpunished. (Proverbs 17:5)

> If your enemy is hungry, give him food to eat; if he is thirsty, give him water to drink. In doing this, you will heap burning coals on his head, and the Lord will reward you. (Proverbs 25:21, 22)

"I can think whatever I want"—have you heard that line? Have you ever said it yourself? Well, if you're a Christian, God has every right to tell you what to think. And He says that an "it's-about-time-he-got-his-just-deserts" attitude is wrong.

You are not to celebrate the downfall of another. Instead, your part is to help that undeserving person. Your unexpected kindness, like coals of fire, can burn into the conscience and melt even the worst animosity—and so turn an enemy into a friend. Don't just light that fire but put some coals on it like turning the other cheek, returning good for evil, and blessing the person who cursed you.

Once you've experienced the miracle of receiving God's power and love to turn an enemy into a friend, revenge will seem totally childish.

🖎 Rethinking the Situation

Mallory came home from school thinking, *If Shauna thinks she's going to slip back in with us just as if nothing happened, I'm going to give her a piece of my mind.* Her conscience *was* bothering her, but she had no intention of giving in.

Getting ready for bed, she was secretly glad she was reading through the book of Exodus. She thought that none of the laws of Moses would give her any conviction. But to her surprise she read, "If you come across your enemy's ox or donkey wandering off, be sure to take it back to him. If you see the donkey of someone who hates you fallen down under its load, do not leave it there; be sure you help him with it" (Exodus 23:4, 5).

It might as well have said, "Just because Shauna has given you the cold shoulder and acted superior, don't refuse to let her back into the 'Plain Jane Club.' "

"All right, God," Mallory conceded, "I'm sorry. My attitude is wrong. I *will* love Shauna and help her return to you."

The next day at lunch, a tearful Shauna pleaded with them to forgive her and to let her sit with them. Mallory put her arm around her, "We love you," she comforted, "and so does God."

Two weeks later, Shauna gave her testimony at the Christian club meeting. She explained that God had pardoned her for hurting her friends. Then she apologized to everyone for her wrong attitudes and asked their forgiveness.

She said, "I'm so thankful for Christians who act like Jesus. I was so discouraged, and I thought I'd ruined my whole life. I'd decided that if my Christian friends wouldn't accept me back, then probably God would never forgive me. I was thinking maybe I should commit suicide."

Mallory shuddered. She had come so close to taking revenge, but the Holy Spirit had touched and changed her heart.

☛ Putting the Truth Into Practice

Is there someone you're tempted to get even with? Ask God how you can specifically apply Luke 6:27 and 28.

1. "Love your enemies."

    Lord, replace my resentment with your never-ending love. In my own strength I can't even tolerate_____. I give up my rights and constantly receive by faith the miracle of your love.

2. "Do good to those who hate you."

    God, show me what I can do to show my love to _____, who is trying to make my life miserable. Give me a special chance to help that person when he or she has problems.

3. "Bless those who curse you."

    Lord, I'm willing to do/say only good things about_____ and appreciate his/her good points.

4. "Pray for those who mistreat you."

    Dear God, I'm willing to pray for_____every day.

    (Secret: You can't hate someone you constantly pray for.)

Self-Examination

Part V: The Terrible Trio: Pride, Rash Actions, Revenge—and Review

ACROSS:

1. One problem caused by disobeying God's rules regarding sex.
2. The devil provokes _____ action because he loves to see people suffer.
6. Instead of always thinking of your point of view _____ yourself in another's position.
8. Solomon, the _____ wise guy.
10. Common preposition.
13. Conjunction.
15. Do not " _____ in the seat of mockers" (Psalm 1:1).
17. "Bless them that _____ you" (Matt. 5:44, KJV).

19. Laziness is very _____ - _____ .
22. Used for cutting down trees during pioneer days.
23. Extracted from a mine.
25. Common suffix.
26. One of four directions.
27. New _____ thinking is completely contrary to the Bible.
28. You can live victoriously because "the one who is in you is _____ than the one who is in the world" (1 John 4:4).
29. God has chosen to reveal himself through Sacred _____ found in the Bible.
30. Lazy people fail to plan _____ .
31. Unforgiveness brings bitterness instead of _____ .
34. Failure to obey God brings serious _____ .
38. Accept the _____ in your life like your looks and your family.
42. To receive inner healing you must be ready to _____ .
43. _____ first the kingdom of God and other things shall be added to you.
45. One boy who learned to conquer laziness.
46. Truth does *not* come from _____ .
48. Do not rejoice at another's _____ .
50. All your _____ friends should be Christians.
51. The idea that you have a divine nature is a _____ .
52. Don't _____ God for the consequences of your sin.

DOWN

1. _____ that contradicts the Bible is dangerous to your spiritual health.
3. In _____ your ways, acknowledge Him.
4. God only uses people who are _____ enough to realize that they need Him every minute.
5. Popular pet.
6. _____ comes before destruction.
7. Bless those who _____ you.
9. Noise made by a horn.
11. God forbids _____ outside of marriage.
12. It is very difficult to stand against _____ pressure, especially if your good friends are non-Christians.
14. The Bible forbids taking personal _____ .
16. Losing a Christian friend is a _____ .
18. _____ time for dates with Jesus.
20. When you accomplish something important, be sure you give God the _____ .
21. The Lord _____ s all the proud of heart.

24. There is great ____ to be found in God's Word.
32. You can solve many problems on your ____ in prayer.
33. ____ without knowledge is not good. (Proverbs 19:2)
35. Pride breeds many a ____ .
36. Laziness is ____ .
37. Jesus is the ____ of Christianity.
39. When you realize that you're wrong, you must ____ .
40. Before making important decisions, seek ____ from mature Christians.
41. A good friend can keep a ____ .
44. The lazy person in Proverbs claimed that this animal roamed the streets.
46. Made by a spider.
47. Abbreviation used in printing that means next line.
49. Exodus says that if your enemy's ____ wanders off, you are to bring it back to him.

(Solution on page 240)